★ ——————————————

The door wasn't locked. It wasn't even latched. I fell forward into the living room and threw my arms out to catch my fall, but my own weight sent me barreling to the floor. My solar plexus hit something soft and hard at the same time. When I opened my eyes I was staring into the face of Mrs. Berkowitz, her scrabbly, gnarled fist curled under my abdomen. I pushed away, and got to a crawl position, struggling to make sense of what I saw.

There she was, the old lady of the underworld, legs splayed out in a V, her plaid skirt up to her thighs, exposing her bitty, round knees. Her eyes were wide-open, and so was her mouth. Her arms were out in a relaxed "I give" fashion, and it didn't take a doctor, or even a doctor's wife, to spot the obvious. The German clock announced the hour then, and I couldn't help but say aloud, "Ding-dong—the Witz is dead."

—————————— ★ ——————————

Death for Dessert

T. Dawn Richard

TORONTO • NEW YORK • LONDON
AMSTERDAM • PARIS • SYDNEY • HAMBURG
STOCKHOLM • ATHENS • TOKYO • MILAN
MADRID • WARSAW • BUDAPEST • AUCKLAND

To my mother, Mary Helen Wallace—a woman who can find humor in just about everything.

DEATH FOR DESSERT

A Worldwide Mystery/March 2007

First published by Five Star.

ISBN-13: 978-0-373-26595-4
ISBN-10:   0-373-26595-6

Printed in U.S.A.

Acknowledgments

Many people have, in one way or another, had a part in seeing that this book was written. My agents, Robert Brown and Sharene Martin, believed in my ability as a writer. Glenn Richard, my husband, spent many cold nights alone while I pounded the keys into the wee hours of the morning. Calin, Summer, Genny and Jesse, my children, encouraged me along the way and laughed at all of the appropriate lines. Bob Parks, my e-mail writing buddy, cheered me on. Bob Youney gave me courage. Mannon Wallace, my father, was steadfastly confident. Tina, Heather, Lee and Mark, my siblings, waited patiently. My editor, John Helfers, looked after me with a discerning eye and a gentle pen. And finally, the Spokane Writers Guild and Ruby's Writers provided invaluable assistance while offering gentle, constructive criticism.

ONE

I SUPPOSE I shouldn't have waited three days before telling someone old Mrs. Berkowitz in Apartment 3C was dead, but I had my reasons. After all, it should have been me getting all the attention, what with a fancy schmansy funeral and weeping and such, because I was supposed to have been the corpse on the couch, not old Mrs. Berkowitz.

Maybe I'm getting ahead of myself. Maybe I should begin at the beginning, and then you can decide whether or not I did the right thing. The truth be known, now I'm not so sure.

It all started when my doctor husband of thirty-five years made it clear that he preferred silicone to cellulite and high heels to bunions. Out you go, May Bell! Make way for Ginger, or Tasha, or whoever the heck the girl *du jour* happened to be. So I went, but not before I lovingly filled his gas tank with sugar, unselfishly scorch-pressed his shirts and scrubbed the toilets, careful to put his toothbrush back in the little holder after I'd finished. So now I'm on my own. The only thing I can fit into my cleaned-out savings account and cancelled credit card budget is an Active Senior Living apartment complex, in a town as far from my life as I could get. I came to understand *active* meant who could grab the first bagel at free bread day or who could stamp a Bingo card with the biggest flourish. Yawn.

I'm in Apartment 3D. I share a stairwell with a senile old man who wanders around the grounds shouting out, "What? What?" He's in Apartment 3B and wears hip waders when he's out. His name is Bob.

Then there's a couple downstairs who enjoy mariachi tunes at 5 a.m. They have a dog named Paco who speaks yapanese. The dog complains about the music, but nobody does anything about it. They live in 3A.

That leaves Mrs. Berkowitz. The first time I saw her she was peeking through her open door watching me muscle a typewriter up the stairs. I, being brought up proper, lifted a hand to wave a hello and the blasted typewriter saw an opportunity to escape. I jumped out of the way because it began its descent directly at my toe. I began my own backwards tumble shortly thereafter. I was a goner for sure, until something soft bounced me forward and I realized—pardon me while I cringe—that I had rebounded off the gelatinous belly of Mr. Bob, Apartment 3B. He shouted, "What? What?" and turned to resume his wanderings, not interested, after all, in the newcomer. Mrs. Berkowitz cackled loudly and closed her door with a shuddering slam. The flesh under my arms quivered a full five seconds while I stood, trying to decide if I should recover the dented typewriter or restore my dignity. I chose the latter.

The apartment I was assigned was your typical fare, with the personality of a soured milk carton. If I had been thirty years younger, maybe I could have imagined things to give it breath, like swatches, or glazes, or mohair. But seeing this as a mere transitory state, I thrust whatever belongings weren't in storage hither and yon.

And there I was, settled in.

The first night was blisteringly hot. I made a mental note to buy a box fan. I stared at the ceiling wearing nothing but T-shirt and panties, working hard to keep my lumpity varicose veins from touching. I was dewy all over and for a while regretted letting the house go, with its ceiling fans and central everything. I assured my husband that I had prepaid the mortgage. I wish I could have seen his face when he got the foreclosure notice, or his surprise when he tried to use his credit cards on Tasha or Tiffany or whoever yanked his crank for the moment.

I missed him.

Maybe that's when I lost my mind. Maybe it was when the girl thing started. I can't remember exactly, but first I was there and the next thing I know I'm doing things I couldn't even imagine I would do. It happens to the best of us.

THE FIRST MORNING in my new home was, glory be, Bread Day! I answered a rapid knock at my door.

The mariachi couple presented themselves, a tiny brown man and his even smaller wife, all smiles. I was distracted for a minute by a glinting gold tooth tucked away behind Mr. Mariachi's wide upper lip.

"Here, for you!"

Mrs. Mariachi held out a bulge of something wrapped in foil. I accepted the present, feeling the leakage around the seams. I tried my best to return the smile while restraining the urge to wipe my hands.

"Free bread day. Don't be late or the best stuff will be gone."

Mr. Mariachi wagged his finger by his hairline and took his wife's elbow.

"Welcome, welcome!" She called out as they stepped in tandem down the stairs.

I pushed the door closed with my foot and ran the package over to the counter before it dripped on the carpet, not that anyone would have noticed. There was a peculiar, yet familiar smell climbing up the walls to the ceiling. So I poked open the foil with my fingernail. Tamales swimming in enough garlic to strip paint—yum. Time to venture out.

The Senior Center was alive with warm bodies maneuvering for prime positions. A table was covered with mounds of yeast products and bagels, expiration dates questionable. There was a commotion in the potted plant corner, so I was grateful for the opportunity to slip into the hubbub without drawing attention as fresh blood. It was Mr. Bob What-What, standing in black rubber boots and nothing else. His back was to me, thank goodness, but this only meant I had an unobscured view of his buttocks, sagging like deflated balloons.

A red-faced woman who I recognized as April Fleet, the Apartment Manager, was trying her best to hold a fern over his front, but Bob was determined to muscle his way past her on his way to the muffins. I couldn't help but notice his stomach, the one that had saved the day for me, all white and bulging, swallowing his naval whole. I shifted my eyes before seeing anything farther south. The manager whispered loudly in his ear and Bob shouted back, "What? What?" before relenting and heading back, assisted, to his apartment.

"Don't let him bother you, dearie," a woman said, and then touched her bony fingers to my arm. Her face was corrugated with lipstick painted red and shiny, high up over the lip line. "At least today he was wearing boots." She giggled and tried to cover it with her hand, which, when she removed it, had slid her lipstick over onto one cheek.

"Oh," was all I could manage. What I really wanted more than anything was to get the heck out of there. The crowd pulsed forward, though, so I found myself in front of the table and I just grabbed at whatever I could find.

"Good choice!" Mr. Mariachi said, his gold tooth winking like a beacon. "Bran. Can't get enough bran."

Mrs. Mariachi nodded vigorously. I looked down at my package, a four-pack of bran muffins freckled with raisins. The name on the package was *Smooth Sailin'*. Lord deliver us.

By the time I got back to my apartment, the temperature had reached at least 200 degrees, I was certain of it. The smell of tamales made me feel green, so I went about throwing open the windows. I shoved the balcony door open as well, and gulped fresh air from the deck. Then, I three-bagged the tamales, looked both ways before making my dash, and gave them a proper burial in the Dumpster at the end of the sidewalk. I made myself a mental note to tell the Mariachis how wonderful they tasted.

Mrs. Berkowitz was watching me again as I huffed and puffed at the top of the stairs. I could see her door open just a crack, her one eye pressed against the wood.

"Hello!" I said, but she slammed the door again. This time her cackling laugh was muffled but just as clear and just as eerie as before.

I spent the day sorting, sweating, and wondering how I could break my lease. Six months seemed interminable. It's temporary, I reminded myself. *Temporary.* But the idea of spending months there felt like forever, and by that evening I was starved. I regretted throwing away the tamales and considered going on a Dumpster forage, but resorted to a Clark bar and 7-Up from the machine downstairs. I sat on my porch to enjoy my feast and escape the heat. Unfortunately, there was one thing I couldn't escape.

"Gonna rain, I think." Mr. Mariachi was craning his

neck from downstairs, smiling and leaning out over his mock-porch railing until I though he might just cartwheel right over. Sort of wished he would. The gold tooth looked orange in the dusky light. Being proper, I smiled back and tipped my soda can at him.

"Yes, it does look like rain." The air smelled wet, and I prayed for anything to take the heat off. Rain would be just the ticket.

"Say. Why don't they have air conditioning in these apartments? Mine is simply blistering."

Mr. Mariachi continued to stare at me, so I searched for something to take his attention off my legs. Lumpity or not, they seemed particularly interesting to the little brown man.

"No air. No, no air." Mariachi shook his head. What in the world was that supposed to mean anyway? I began to get irritated. I just wanted a moment of peace, and he was still grinning up while shoving and shifting to get a better look. I started to say something dismissive, when I heard a commotion across the way. Peering through the dim stairwell light, I caught a glimpse of Mrs. Berkowitz and, this time, I was determined to get some kind of response. Call me stubborn, but remember I was irritated and hot. Bad combination.

"Hello there!" I stood and leaned over the deck similar to what Mr. Mariachi was doing while waving my free hand. Mrs. Berkowitz turned quickly and froze, her white face an oval of undistinguishable features, glowing in the shadows.

"I'm your new neighbor, May List. What's your name?" I felt like a schoolgirl at camp. If she didn't answer me, I was prepared to throw pillows.

She answered. "When are you going to get that confounded typewriter off the landing?"

I was caught off guard. "I, uh, well," duh… Great, May Bell, let's be eloquent.

"Get it off!" She shouted, and then slid back through her balcony door. I waited for the cackle. This time, however, it was Mr. Mariachi snorting as if it were all some kind of joke.

"She some piece of work," he huh-huhed. "Nobody see her much. Not even bread day. But when you do, stay clear. She some piece of work."

Mr. Mariachi laughed all the way back into his apartment and, at that moment, I didn't feel like sitting outside anymore. Besides, fat raindrops were plunking down, so I closed up for the night and went to bed.

TWO

I WOKE UP three hours later. Don't know why, I just lay there wide-awake and, no matter how hard I tried, sleep wasn't coming. At least I didn't have to listen to festive music or frustrated dogs. All was quiet at the loony bin. I found a book and stared at its pages for a while. It's a well-known fact that gloomy emotions are strongest in the middle of the night, and I started feeling sorry for myself. This wasn't the way things were supposed to be. I should have been home in bed with my husband and my itty-bitty book light. I didn't have those things anymore, so I threw back the sheet and visited the refrigerator. I needed a little something to take my mind off Poor Me.

At first, I thought the noise was the icemaker. Then I remembered I didn't have an icemaker. I stopped with my hand on the cupboard and listened. There! A scratchy, bumping from outside, close enough to my door to give me the shakes.

Cats maybe. I'd seen them prowling and slinking along the complex foundations, dispassionate feral beasts, probably working over my surrendered tamales.

Thud.

That was no cat. Maybe it was a crack maniac, too long between victims and desperate to satisfy his sinful passions. I held my breath and tiptoed over to the front door; thankful I'd remembered to hook the safety chain. I pressed my eye to the peephole. Imagine my astonishment! Old Mrs. Berkowitz, her back pressed against the landing wall between her apartment and mine, was shoving my typewriter toward the stairs with her bare feet. As she inched the machine along, I could see strain on her face. Her eyes said she was on a mission.

"What are you doing?" I yelled as I threw open the door, no longer worried about rapists or beasties. "That's my typewriter. What do you think you're doing?"

She didn't seem surprised in the least. She didn't even flinch or offer a lame excuse, just pushed harder and faster. Her bottom was now inches above the landing floor, her palms flattened against the wall. Her nightgown had ridden above knees that looked like golf balls under tissue paper.

"There!" She exclaimed, and, as she gave the final heroic push, her feet shot out from under her, sending the typewriter airborne. It flew along, hitting every other step before coming to rest, in pieces, just north of Bob What-What's apartment. The clamor rattled the windows. Paco started, but after a yap or two, he was silent.

I stood with my arms reaching helplessly for my battered machine, too astonished to utter a word. Mrs. Berkowitz struggled to her feet, her look of smug satisfaction a slap in my face. She brushed her hands, and then punched her knuckles against her hips, elbows out.

"It had to go," she said.

I was still trying to find my voice. Maybe I was in the grip of a lucid dream. I pushed my fingernails into my palms—deep. Ouch! Nope, this was for real.

"Why did you do that?" I asked, waiting for an answer and sure I wouldn't get one. Then a door opened downstairs and Bob lumbered out, wearing nothing but a life preserver. "What? What?" he shouted at the typewriter. Mrs. Berkowitz cackled, lifting the hair on the back of my neck.

"Couldn't sleep, could yah?" she asked, her jarring laughter ending like she'd been dunked.

"Just getting a glass of water," I said and wondered if I'd ever sleep again.

"Sure. A glass of water. Well, I suppose now's as good a time as any to make our acquaintance, so get on in here." With that, she turned her back, walked through her door, and motioned me to follow.

"No it's late," I started, "I have a lot to do tomorrow."

The old woman turned slightly. When she looked back over her shoulder, her eyes told me she didn't believe a thing I'd said. From what I'd observed already, nobody here had a lot to do tomorrow, or any day for that matter. What the heck. I followed her in.

"Sit." Mrs. Berkowitz pointed to a sofa, and I sat. I was prepared for the fetch command, but instead she said, "I'll fix the tea. You just wait there."

I watched from my perch, feeling more and more uncomfortable, yet silly at the same time. This was a harmless, lonely, old woman needing company. I'd heard that old people sleep less and less until they just never sleep, probably holding on to every last second.

Her apartment was a backwards double of mine and while it seemed normal, the closer I looked, the more I realized, that things were anything but normal. She had expensively framed pictures on the walls, nailed in exact patterns, hanging upside down. Little Boy Blue was standing on his head. A small aquarium hummed lazily with bubbles popping on the surface of water. There was a tiny scuba diver and treasure chest sunk into the rocky bottom but there were no fish. A phone lay by my hand with the coil unplugged and wrapped tightly around the receiver. On a shelf, she had a collection of dusty books, but there were no ▓▓▓ ▟▟ ▓▓ spines.

"You should have gotten rid of that old portable a long time ago. Ain't yah ever heard of computers?" Mrs. Berkowitz startled me when she returned with two china teacups. Mine was chipped by the handle, but I drank around it as I struggled to make sense of what was absolutely senseless. I made an effort to look comfortable as I wondered what kind of tea I was drinking, its flavor as odd as everything else in her place.

"My son set me up years ago." I watched her pinch her lips together. They drew down into the tea and slurped, as she squinted at me through the steam.

"That's nice," I said, wishing I could drink the hot tea faster.

"Oh, no. You think I have a little word processor or something. When I say he set me up, I mean he *set me up!*" Mrs. Berkowitz's eyes twinkled, but not in a charming way. The twinkle was more a flicker of something not said, a warning that I couldn't figure out. I felt a strange sensation in my stomach and set the tea on the doily-covered coffee table. The doily wasn't a doily in the traditional sense, but a pair of lace gloves being used as a coaster. Mrs. Berkowitz sat across from me, drawing from her cup, staring like she expected me to say something. So I did.

"You have beautiful hair," I said. It was the truth. She had the most perfectly placed curls back-combed into a fluffy gray ball. At this, her screamed laughter caused me to jump, banging my shins in the process, on the underside of her coffee table. I thought of our downstairs neighbor shouting, "What? What?" as Mrs. Berkowitz grabbed her hair and lifted it six inches above her head. With her free hand she patted her now bare scalp and crowed, "Bald as an onion!"

Put that thing back on! I wanted to shout, but I just sat there rubbing my ankles, while she expertly replaced her rug and smoothed the sides. Good as new.

"Thank you so much for the tea, but I'm getting really sleepy. I think I'd better just go home." I could feel a nervous flush creeping up my front. My upper lip was moist the way it gets when I sit naked in the doctor's office, or in the dentist chair (not naked of course), or any place I felt a desperate need to escape.

Mrs. Berkowitz's mouth pulled down into a frown. I watched, transfixed, as her deep blue eyes turned steely gray. I must have made her angry. I was getting the feeling that was something you shouldn't do to Mrs. Berkowitz. What had Mr. Mariachi said? *She some piece of work! Stay clear!*

"Why didn't you kick him out?" Mrs. Berkowitz asked. Gone was the friendly old neighbor lady. She leaned forward in her chair and her eyes narrowed.

"I beg your pardon?" Now the place between my breasts was beading up. Soon there would be a trickle.

Her voice had lowered, sounding raspy like a woman who'd smoked a lot of Winstons over the years. "You know who I'm talking about. And I know you know."

A swarm of flies began buzzing in my head. The room dipped sharply to the left. I was scared. Not just nervous, scared. The old lady looked right into me with her eyes, now pale and milky, like the color had just leaked out.

"I really have to go," I squeaked. I stood too quickly and banged my shins again on that damnable coffee table as I scooted toward the door. I half expected Mrs. Berkowitz to lunge forward, blocking my path, but she just sat there, her cheeky smile pasted back on her face as she patted her hair with a liver-spotted hand.

"You go then, Sugar, but you'll be coming back," she said, like a kindly old aunt giving advice, "and when you do, I'll be waiting for an answer."

I got to my apartment in a hurry. My hands shook so bad I fumbled the chain, dropped it, scrambling to get it into the notch. I threw the deadbolt and stood with my back to the door. When my breathing returned to normal, I went to the sink for that glass of water. My hands were still shaking so badly though, that most of it went down my front. It didn't matter; it felt good, actually. There was a veritable waterfall coursing its way down the gorge as it was. I needed a shower.

THREE

BACK IN BED I stretched out across the covers in my sopping wet P.J.'s with the notion that if I lay there wet and dripping, a breeze would come and cool me down. No breeze tonight, so I dripped and reminded myself that tomorrow I'd buy a fan. I rubbed my naked wedding band finger and stared at the ceiling.

Things that usually made life easier hadn't worked this time—not the shower, the box of Raisinettes or the bag of Cheetos. I just couldn't shake the roiling unease robbing me of sleep. I watched the green digits on my clock tick off the minutes, and felt the rumble as a train rolled along. It sounded like it was rolling right through the parking lot, and I hoped the vibration was a train, not an earthquake, and I wished I were anywhere but there.

Why didn't you kick him out?

Had that old woman really said that? I tried every combination of words, trying to come up with some sensible alternative to what I thought I'd heard.

Why didn't you stick it out? Maybe she'd seen my pinkie indelicately coiled while I sipped her tea. *My isn't it sticky out?* It was hot, dreadfully so. *Fly did a chicken shout!* Ridiculous. No, she'd said it. *Why didn't you kick him out?*

She had said the very thing I had thought every minute of every day since I'd left my husband. Why didn't I kick *him* out? After all, I had good reason to believe he had bedded at least one nurse at his hospital right there in the O.B. ward. Don't think for a minute she hadn't found good use for those stirrups. Maybe those starry-eyed candy stripers and helium-headed catheter jockeys needed his blessings and affectionate squeezes to say, *Ya done good Steffy, now let me show you my appreciation,* but not me. No, I could make it on my own. Stand on my own two bunions, thank you very much.

Why didn't you kick him out?

She knew. The strange old upside down, glove-doily, no-hair woman across the landing knew, and it was giving me the creeps. It shouldn't have, you might think. Word travels fast around a place like Active Senior Living complexes, but I had told no one about my life. No one. I had wiped the slate clean. I even gave the cat away before I left, and the only thing I had taken with me was my name. I'd left anything else suggesting a hint of who I'd been a thousand miles behind. *But she knew. Somehow she knew.*

Despite the smothering heat, I shivered when an icy finger ran along my spine. Goose bumps punched up through my skin, caused by an alarming awareness that she had been able to invade my privacy in a most disconcerting way.

The clock ticked off another minute as the train sounds faded away and Paco barked twice, but all I heard was her voice.

Why didn't you kick him out?

I wondered what my husband was doing. It wasn't healthy, thinking about stuff that twisted my stomach into knots, but the thoughts seemed to creep in, and for once I didn't shoo them away—anything to shake off the memory of Mrs. Berkowitz now hovering around me like residual tamale vapors.

"Nurse Bambie! We've got an emergency in here. Start this woman on lactating ringers."

"But Doctor, don't you mean lactated ringers?"

"What did I say? Oh, silly me. Yes, lactated ringers, and I'll need a chest X-ray pronto."

"But Doctor she has a broken femur!"

"Broken female? I mean femur? My, my yes. Her leg looks very long—I mean wrong! I suppose I'll need to palpate her thigh."

"Palpate her thigh?"

"To see if she has a pulse, of course, you know; check her arteries."

"Doctor List, she's slapping you. Don't you think that's a pretty sure sign she has a pulse?"

"I'll say she's stacked, I mean, she packs a wallop, but you never can tell about these things; she can go any minute. Just let me get a good feel here, I mean, a good position on the body..."

"Doctor List! There's nothing wrong with her heart!"

"I should say not. It's thudding like a jack-hammer under my hands. Better do a full examination. Nurse! The rubber gloves!"

I laughed out loud in spite of myself. What a sot. A quart of Very Berry ice cream finally cleared the bad taste from my mouth. I drifted off eventually, dry and full-belly happy, when the clock slid its numbers over to 3:00.

THE TYPEWRITER was gone from the bottom of the stairs the next morning. I suppose some enterprising mechanic salvaged the thing, or maybe Mr. Greenjeans, the maintenance guy, scooped it up. I'd seen him puttering around the day of my grand tour. He'd been outfitted in tool-laden, olive green coveralls, working his fingers over an ailing azalea bush. He moved away when we approached, avoiding the inevitable introduction, with the type of lurching, hunched gait that was typical of most of the active residents. I guessed his age, though, to be more in the mid-forty range.

"He's a little simple." Ms. Fleet had said, sounding apologetic, during my facility tour.

"He appears quite capable," I said. It was one of those comments that dribbles out of my mouth, always the cheery, glass-is-half-full type of woman, when what I really wanted to say was, *Oh yeah, missing a chromosome? Elevator stops at the second floor?*

Mensa challenged? while drawing a ring around my ear. But I didn't say those things because I'm nice, and I was brought up proper.

"Oh, yes. Quite capable. Good word. Now here we are! The laundry room. And isn't it beautiful?"

That had been my grand tour. Since then, I'd seen Mr. Greenjeans slinking around quite a bit, once holding the tail of a lifeless brown mouse, looking as if he were considering putting it in his pocket.

Maybe he did.

FOUR

I WAS A LITTLE SAD to lose my typewriter. I'd wanted
to try my hand at writing for years, and once I'd left
my husband there were no more excuses. That typewriter was going to be my inspiration. After all, how
can you look at a nice, clean sheet of white paper
waving in the grasp of an IBM Selectric, without
hearing it call for something brilliant to fly from the
keys? Merry May would think of something, even
longhand, if need be, but I didn't have a clue as to what
I would write. That was depressing and debilitating. I
had to push away the *who do you think you're kidding*
thoughts, and get on with my life.

"May Flower! Where is my little May Flower?" I
stopped on my way to the bathroom. The voice was
muted, like it was straining through time and matter.
"May Flower!"

I could hardly breathe. It was a sweet little title my
husband had given me while we were dating. Later it
became a nuisance, grating on my ears when he would
come home two hours later than promised. While
dinner burned on the stove, he would sing, "May
Flower, where are you?"

The cackle followed. My hands began to tingle when a shot of adrenaline shattered my nervous system. It wasn't enough that the old hag somehow knew that I had left my husband. Now she taunted me with personal, impossible-to-know stuff. I raced to the bathroom and slammed the door, reminiscent of my first encounter with Mrs. Berkowitz. This time, my whole body was vibrating long after the walls shuddered to a stop.

I crammed my fingers into my ears, and tried to wiggle out of my pajama bottoms doing a poor imitation hula dance. I really had to go now, and by the time I gave up on my dance and grabbed the waistband with my hands, I didn't care what my ears heard. Either go, or make an unscheduled visit to the laundry room.

Thankfully, the voice was quiet for the duration of my potty break. Then I heard something else that nearly made me scream.

"May Day! May Day! She's goin' down! May Day! Can anyone hear me? What? Nothing I can do? Guess I'll have to bail, then. Here I goooo!"

There was a loud thump, followed by a moment of silence. I wondered if Mrs. Berkowitz had thrown herself over the balcony wall. Then her hyena laugh cut the silence, an assault to my eardrums.

Too bad.

I started pacing. Chinese torture would have been like a massage at this point. Pull out my fingernails, exfoliate my entire body. I heard her door creak open, and I stopped short, staring toward my little safety chain.

She was singing.

Softly, and so low I could barely hear, but she was singing all right, and it was another thing she couldn't have known.

But she did.

"She's making a list, checking it twice, gonna find out if he's naughty or nice, Teddy boy is comin' to town."

The song my husband had crooned in my ear when we were still in love. Usually in the back seat of his Mustang (he always liked muscle cars), the suggestions were clear, and at first cute, but later his little made-up songs were sickening and obscene. I raced to the door on my toes and carefully leaned toward the peephole. Mrs. Berkowitz was staring into my eyes with her pale, leaky, blue ones. I stifled a shriek and pushed off, tangled my feet together and sat down hard. I didn't curse, being brought up proper, but I wanted to.

Ted List, what have you done? The answer was suddenly clear. The apocalyptic thought actually liberated me and drowned out the retreating Berkowitz cackle. That was it! My husband had somehow found me, and had sicced this old woman on me, a macabre ploy meant to drive me straight to Bellevue. I'd seen him angry enough times, and knew what he could do, but this, Teddy boy, was really low. I wasn't afraid anymore. It wasn't a strange Twilight Zone experience, after all, because there was finally an explanation. I could deal with this, and deal with it, I would. After a long, cold shower, a pint of Ben & Jerry's, and a visit to the apartment manager.

April was less than helpful. She hemmed and hawed and squirmed aplenty, but the final analysis was that the complex was full, I couldn't move into another apartment, there was nothing she could do, and if I broke my lease it would be major bucks that I didn't care to squander. However, if there was anything else she could do…

Thanks a lot.

On my way back to purgatory, I spotted the pool and changed course. I could use a heel dip about then, and I wanted to know more about my bald neighbor. There was the arrangement of recognizable faces and languishing bodies sprawled around on the tile or in the reclining pool chairs. I hadn't seen so much skin in my entire life. And when I say skin, I mean there was at least a football field of it, if you stretched out all the wrinkles. It's really interesting how much space you can save by folding flesh over a few times.

"May! May List! Get on over here honey, there's someone I want you to meet."

I worked my face into a smile and nodded at the woman shielding her eyes. Mrs. Gateway, the welcoming committee. I had one of her handmade potholders hanging on my fridge, and I hadn't even been there a week. What the heck. Maybe if I played a bit dense, I could squeeze some information out of her. She was the type of gal who could be cheerful during an IRS interrogation. Seeing how she wasn't shy about knowing everyone and everything that was going on around the place, she might be an important resource.

There was a tremendous splash off to my left, and I was showered with half the pool. The beach party roared with applause, encouraging Mrs. Cook, now climbing up the steps looking proud. She plucked at the elastic around her dimpled thighs.

"Nice cannonball, Joyce!" some old guy I didn't know yelled out, with a thumbs-up. That made her happy.

"You're drenched!" Mrs. Gateway cried. "Doesn't it feel good? So refreshing."

"Like a spring shower." I squeezed the hem of my skirt, making as if it was nothing at all. My hair was mashed to one wet side of my head. "I just planned to get my feet in, but, well, this is so much better."

"Look out! There she goes again!" Another thunderclap before a mushroom cloud of spray blew into the air, hung there for a minute, and then the umbrella fell over the crowd. I gave up on the skirt. More applause, more cheers; the water level was down at least a foot.

"I think she gave it her everything that time," Mrs. Gateway exclaimed, flapping her hands together, like a zoo seal. "She'll need to take a breather after that one."

"That's too bad. There's a patch on my left shoulder still dry," I murmured.

Mrs. Gateway smacked the chair beside her. Water splashed. "This one's empty."

"So tell me," I needed a way to break the ice, "how

long have you lived here?" I settled into the puddle, and stretched my legs out. The water started getting warm under my bottom. Not too bad if I didn't shift.

"She's been here forever." The thumbs-up man sauntered over and winked at Mrs. G. "I think she may have been born here."

"Don't encourage Grady. He's been trying to get me in the sack for years." Mrs. Gateway threw a towel at Thumbs-Up, and told him to cover his bony shoulders.

"Got my new prescription, Ida!" The thumb went up again, along with another lingering wink, his mouth pulled down at the corner. "Viagra. Full strength. I'll take two if you go out on a date with me."

"Why don't you go out with your thumb?" Mrs. Gateway pretended to play hard to get, but I could sense she was more than a little curious about the Viagra possibilities. The pink in her cheeks was too immediate to be sunburn.

I tried to draw the conversation back around to something useful.

"It's nice here," I lied. "Everyone has been very friendly, but I don't know anyone very well yet."

"Don't you worry, you'll make friends soon enough." Ida patted my arm. "You've only been here a few days."

"What about you? Are you from California originally?" I was struggling, wanting to get to Mrs. Berkowitz, but didn't want to sound too eager.

"Oh, yes! I was a fourth grade teacher for twenty-five years. Raised a house full of kids. They all wanted me to come live with them after I retired, but I said no thank you. Can you imagine? Changing poopie diapers all day long? I've got enough just to keep up with these darned Depends things." She pulled at her bathing suit, and it was all I could do not to say "Oooee!" I changed my mind about going for a swim any time soon.

Another roar went up from the opposite side of the pool. Bob What-What had come through the gate with the apartment manager in harried pursuit. He had on a thong. Not a little disappearing bathing suit, a thong. One orange flip-flop on his left foot, and nothing else. Ms. Fleet grabbed up a towel and started flinging it out like she was trying to lasso a calf. When that didn't work, she hugged him from behind, and gave him a terry cloth skirt.

"What? What?" He yelled at everyone, braying at poolside. The manager pinched the towel at his lower back, and pulled him away. Everyone clapped and hooted.

"That's Bob. I'm sure you've seen him around."

"A little more of him than I would like."

"He was the San Dimas fire chief for years. He gets all the doughnuts on free bread day if you're not fast," Ida said.

"I ought to slip him a few of my Viagras," Grady said. "Then he could bring us coffee and doughnuts at the same time."

"Filthy old man!" Mrs. Gateway hit Grady with her rubber swim cap.

"What about you?" I shifted. Darn, the water was cold on that side. "Are you from California, Grady?" These people were a far cry from the friends in my other life. I had a sudden hilarious desire to invite Bob and Grady to my Wednesday morning Bible study. The ladies would probably suffocate on their own vapors.

"Oh no, no. I just came down here because of all the pretty ladies. I heard there were ten gals to every man in this part of the country. I lived most my life in Sandpoint, Idaho. Slim pickin's there, unless you like the type of gal who can overhaul your engine and shoot tobaccy ten feet."

"Well, there's something to be said about those kind, I suppose." Ida squirted a blob of white sunscreen into her hand.

"Help you with that?" Grady reached his hand out and got it slapped.

"I have some interesting neighbors." Here I go, I thought. "A cute Hispanic couple, I think their dog's name is Paco."

"Barks all the time," Mrs. Gateway said. "That's Anita and Marco Ramirez."

"And Bob."

"Who could use a little Viagra," Grady chuckled.

"And Mrs. Berkowitz."

Time stood still for a long second. Ida stopped rubbing in lotion, Grady's thumb withered, and a trio of women off to our right stopped talking. The whole darn pool party looked like it had been rained on.

Mrs. Gateway twisted the cap on her lotion with deliberate, a-bit-too-hard twists, and then she twisted the other way, and opened the bottle again.

"She doesn't get out much. She keeps to herself a lot. Best leave it that way." Her face had changed into a dark cloud. I got the message. This was a conversation closed. But I'm not the type to give up easily. At least not anymore. I'd left that woman back in Ohio.

"What's her story? Has she been here long? Where is she from? I was thinking about getting to know her a little better. Does she have family?" I threw out a veritable barrage of questions, thinking they would answer at least one just to ward off the verbal artillery.

Grady stood, and I caught a look exchange between them as he glanced down at Mrs. Gateway. "Best do as Ida says. Leave it alone." He stepped over to the pool and bent at the waist, then slid into the water. A perfect arrow slicing the surface.

"Listen." Ida leaned toward me. "Nobody knows for sure, but there's rumor that she has connections."

"Connections?"

"Her family is from, uh, let's say somewhere south of Greece or Italy or something. She's got a son, and he comes and goes, mostly at night, but he doesn't talk to anybody. She hangs around that apartment of hers all the time, taking in strange packages. A lot of us think she's got a history, and most of us think it's not completely on the up and out, if you get my drift."

Up and out? Did she mean up and up? I didn't exactly get her drift but I was collecting information, and I wanted more.

"Is she, you know…" I drew a circle around my ear.

"Old Timer's? I think she might want you to believe she's lacking, but she's smart as a whippet. Don't let her fool you. And my advice to you is, keep your distance."

What had Mr. Mariachi said? *She some piece of work! Stay clear!*

I tried a dismissive laugh. "What can she do?" In my mind, though, the collection of events was already haunting me. The songs, the personal details she knew about my life. It was all so strange. Maybe Ted didn't have a hand in this after all.

"You have no idea." Ida picked up the lotion again and squeezed out a palm full of goo. "Make of that what you will."

The pool party seemed a bit less festive then, and I wanted to get out of my wet clothes. I thanked Ida and left through the gate. On my way back to the apartment, I saw Mr. Greenjeans raking leaves. When I glanced over at him, he quickly cast his eyes downward and knelt to examine a patch of dirt, but I knew when my back was to him that he was watching me, because I could feel his eyes like warm probes. It made my wet dress feel all the more transparent.

After an Oreo and root beer snack, I sat on my bed

in panties and bra biting the end of a pencil, listening to the mariachi music, ignoring Paco. I wanted to get on paper some of the things I had learned, because it was a way of passing time, and I was more than a bit intrigued by the reaction of Ida and Grady.

My window was open, so I stayed low, not wanting to give Mr. Greenjeans a free shot. Even though I was sixty-five, I was the youngest chick in the coop and hadn't yet reached full sag.

There was only silence from across the landing, so I presumed Mrs. Berkowitz was either napping or turned to stealth mode. I wasn't about to check the peephole. That would throw off my concentration if her dead fish eyes were peering at me from the other side. I had to think.

I listed the people I knew so far, and what I knew about them.

April Fleet: Apartment manager

Grady Knox: Mr. Thumbs

Ida Gateway: Social butterfly

Mr. and Mrs. Ramirez: AKA the Mariachis

Paco: Yapper

Bob Springer: Mr. What-What

Mr. Greenjeans: Maintenance guy

That brought me to Mrs. Berkowitz. What could I say about her? Strange Ranger. Approx age: eighty-five. Had a thing about typewriters, knew things about me only I should know.

I fanned myself with the notepad while staring at

the ceiling. The temperature in my apartment had leveled off at about ninety degrees, so I decided to cool off in a shower and take a drive.

Before long, I was sitting in the comfort of my recently acquired, air-conditioned Camaro with vanity plates reading STUD DOC. A "gift" from my husband's collection, painted a brilliant candy apple red. The keys had been hanging on the peg beside mine for the Woody Suburban, and I wondered if Ted was enjoying steering that behemoth around parking lots as much as I had. I aimed for a strip mall I'd seen a couple of times.

"MAY I HELP YOU find something?" A young man tapped me on the shoulder, and I wheeled around, pegging a nine on the tension meter. He held his hands up in a defensive posture. His face was dotted with acne, and I couldn't help but notice his hair was an unusual color, a combination pumpkin orange and brown, like a dye job gone awry. The metal ring protruding from one eyebrow made me wince. I couldn't understand why anyone would skewer his body on purpose.

"Um, maybe. I'm looking for a typewriter."

The boy looked at me like I'd asked to see a Victrola. He raised the eyebrow and the ring danced. I winced again.

"Uh, lady…" He pointed to a sign over the cash register. It said *CompUSA*. "The *Comp* means computers. We don't have typewriters here."

"Of course. I knew that." Darn. I tried my best not to look embarrassed but didn't quite pull it off. The boy just stood there. If I'd been drowning he'd probably sit on that stiff, white, inner tube thing and watch.

"Well, then. I guess I need a computer. Something to write with." This perked him up.

"Laptop?"

"I prefer to put it on a desk, I think."

The boy sighed. "PC?"

"I don't know much about brands. Is that a good one?"

The boy rolled his eyes. "Windows enabled?"

I felt a nervous blush creeping, creeping. "Well, they stick sometimes. Really bad in this kind of weather, but if I really get my weight into it…"

"Lady, maybe you should do a little homework before you dump a lot of cashola into one of these things. I can give you some brochures." He sighed again, looking impatient. The ring in his eyebrow was quivering. "Don't you have any grandkids who can help you?"

I think I should have been insulted, but all I could feel at the moment was awkward helplessness. The face of Mrs. Berkowitz as she strained to get my type-writer down to the bottom of the stairs loomed in my mental viewfinder. *Ain't ya ever heard of computers?*

"I'll be back." I shoved the brochures into my purse and left. I needed a Frappuccino from Starbucks to lift my spirits.

I sat on the comfy couch sucking at the icy shake until I got a brain freeze, and pulled the notepad out of my purse. I added a chore list to the apartment dweller details. *Gather data.* Something strange was going on at the Active Senior Living complex, and somehow Mrs. Berkowitz was in the middle of it all. It was the way everyone grew quiet when I mentioned her name. The way Mr. Ramirez had cautioned me away. The way Ida Gateway had said she was involved in things better left alone.

I suppose it was my frozen *medulla oblongata* that did it, or maybe I was past boredom and threw good advice and caution to the wind. Whatever it was, I felt a rebellious courage. I decided right then and there, to go on a more aggressive hunt to *gather data*. Tonight, I would pay Mrs. Berkowitz a visit. I had the excuse I needed folded away in my purse. Tonight, I would get some answers.

FIVE

At first, I didn't recognize the woman standing in Mrs. Berkowitz's doorway. A long-haired brunette appeared after my knock, and gave me a leaky-eyed perusal. It was Mrs. Berkowitz, all right, togged up in wavy tendrils that hung just below her shoulders. To add to her preposterous look, she wore a short, belted, paisley skirt and a cotton white v-neck. She had look-at-me pumps on her feet and sported heavy makeup. Her face was a Picasso of heavy blue eye shadow, tarantula eyelashes, and smudges of eyeliner in thick black coal. I wasn't sure if the brown dot just above her left lip was a faux mole or just an accident. Either way, it wasn't working.

"I knew you'd be back!" The voice was the same, the only reassurance I had this was the old bat, after all. The grating laughter clinched it, and I shook off the blow to my senses before speaking.

"I have some questions about computers and thought maybe you could help me." I held out the brochures like a kid who needed help tying her shoes.

"That I can do, lady, that I can," she said. She grabbed my sleeve, yanked me into her apartment and slammed the door. Nothing she did seemed to be subtle. I wondered for a brief, insane moment if I should have brought my Mace.

"Get on in here." Mrs. Berkowitz took quick, awkward steps toward her bedroom. The spiky heels of her shoes caught in the thick carpet fibers, making the little knotty muscles in her calves expand and contract. From my vantage point she could have been a young girl, but the stoop in her shoulders looked out of place. The whole combination was disturbing.

"What did I tell yah? My son really set me up!"

The things I saw in her bedroom were staggering. Gone were the usual granny accoutrements, replaced by a technological wonderland. Desks, machines, file cabinets, blinking lights, whirring noises, and equipment that I didn't even recognize had taken the place of bed or vanity. I was surprised she didn't have a mirror ball hanging from the ceiling.

She explained. "I use two monitors so's I can access two programs at the same time. I've got tons of gigabytes, super speed, fax, scanner, teleconference capabilities, CD-ROM, hard disks, laser printer, World Wide Web, e-mail, the works."

I could see why she would never have to leave her apartment. She had the universe at her fingertips.

"That's, wow!" I stuttered.

"You just sit down here." She wheeled a chair out and nudged me toward it. With a deft hand she grabbed a little thing she called a mouse, and ran it around on a pad that had the words, *Let's talk at www.Safeway* embossed on its spongy surface. She leaned over my shoulder. The strong smell of Oil of Olay radiated from her skin and made my eyes water. After thirty minutes of demonstrating the dozens of activities her computer could do, my head was pounding, my sinuses were closed, and I was seeing double. It was far more than my brain could handle in one sitting.

"I just want something I can write stories on," I finally said softly, not wanting to sound unappreciative.

"Oh." She sounded hurt. "In that case, just get yourself a monitor and a hard drive and a printer. That should do it. Most computers come with the software you'll need, and with the prices coming down all the time, it shouldn't cost you too much."

Was I being dismissed? I didn't know any more about how to operate one of those wretched machines than I did before. The whole affair had been too over-whelming. Maybe I could visit a pawnshop and find an old typewriter, after all.

"I still don't know how to use it, though." My voice was small.

"I'll tell ya what." Mrs. Berkowitz slid her hair off and wrapped it around her hands. There were a few shimmery, gray leftovers floating around on her scalp. "When you get your computer, just tell the guy in the store what you want to use it for. Get a couple diskettes, then come back over here and I'll help you out."

I felt a bit warmer toward Mrs. Berkowitz. The

bizarre activities over the last two days faded in the light of her generous offering. Then she bent over my shoulder and held her face so close to mine that I could feel her breath.

"Do you have an answer to my question yet?" Her milky eyes were flickering.

I bit back a scream and rolled out of the chair, ducking as I went. I backed toward the door, watching the lights blink at me from the room, pulsing, throbbing, matching my chaotic heart, beat for beat.

"Don't blast a gasket, Maybe Baby." Mrs. Berkowitz straightened, tossed her hair over her shoulder and grinned. Her teeth were wide, ivory chunks, filling her mouth to capacity. They were clean enough. What was I thinking? Why was I even musing about her teeth? That odd, creeping sensation ran up and down my arms again. I didn't care at that minute if I got help with the computer. I didn't care if I *got data,* I just wanted to be in my own bedroom. Under the covers would be good, heat be darned.

I still can't remember how I got away, but instead of going to my apartment, I headed for the stairs. The need to be further away than a skinny landing had my feet moving. As soon as I hit ground level, my legs were scissoring long strides, arms pumping, chin up. Dusk crowded in, turning the sky purple and yellow like a new bruise. Mr. Greenjeans pushed a wheelbarrow full of old newspapers. He stared at them like he was reading when I passed, again avoiding the compulsory "Hello." He needn't have worried. I was on the move.

Some confused architect on a hallucinogen must have designed the apartment complex. Buildings were in no particular pattern that I could tell, pathways weaved in and around them, and a parking lot formed an L shape, keeping it all together. I planned to take a few laps, letting them take me where they would. A solid, mesh fence surrounded the whole labyrinth in a propitious attempt to keep residents in its boundaries, or was it to keep people out? I wasn't sure. Someone had taken the time to plant exquisite gardens. The smell of hyacinths and lavender was heavy, strange company to the stinging odor of Ben Gay and foot powders.

Slowing, I took in row upon row of stacked hovels. Soft light glowed in their identical windows; smells of cooking seeped out; spats of conversation here and there. All the homes were complete with balconies upon which sat the most obnoxious things. There was Mr. Plantman, his balcony tastefully, if not jungle-like, festooned with overflowing vines, ferns and philodendrons. On closer inspection, though, they were all as artificial as Mrs. Berkowitz's coiffures. He was out there now, watering, humming, lifting an arthritic hand to wave. When he smiled at me his dentures shot out, but he was quick with a gnarled fist, and shoved them back in his mouth.

Oooeee.

I just wanted to walk. To shake the dust off my boots

and head home with my hat in hand, nearly ready at that point to share my husband with Tiffany, or Barbie, or whoever. I could swallow my pride, because anything seemed better than this. I was feeling miserably sorry for myself again, and lonely. So lonely, that my thoughts were taking over and I almost didn't hear the familiar voice calling to me from across the way.

"May, Honey, come over here. May List, come join us a spell."

I looked up, straining through the mist that was clouding my vision, looking for a face to go with the voice I'd heard. Tears had begun to pool. I blinked them back.

On the third floor of apartment complex number 15, Mrs. Gateway and Mr. Thumbs hung over the ledge like a couple of coeds. In their hands they held bottles, and as I approached I could see the green glass of Heinekens. Classy. They'd pulled chairs out onto the balcony and hailed me over to join their little party. Somewhere between my apartment and theirs, it had gotten dark. Sprinklers chugged away, crickets started their chorus, and little sidewalk lights gave me a clear path. The effect was pretty and almost resort-like, if I didn't know better.

"Get over here, girlie, before I propose. Save me from a fate worse than death," Mr. Thumbs crowed. Mrs. Gateway jabbed him in the ribs and he spewed a little stream of beer. "One more Heine and I just might," he threatened.

"One more beer, and it will take more than Viagra to get you up in the morning, you old coot!"

"Get your pocketbooks out, ladies, I think I hear a wager!" Grady said.

I climbed the stairs, finding myself wanting their company. However goofy these two were, at least they were fun. I could use a little fun right then.

"Now, May Dear, sit right on out here and let me wait on you a bit." Ida led me to the balcony where I took a white wicker chair with a munificent cushion. She disappeared, and I could hear her humming in her kitchen beyond the screen.

"She'll be getting cookies," Grady said in a whisper. "My advice—don't eat them. Hard as rocks. Look down there." He pointed at bushes on the ground below, and I saw brown dots littering the junipers. I raised my eyebrows. "She's nearsighted and never notices."

"Here we are." Ida came back with a plate of brown dots. "Made them fresh this morning. You just help yourself." She set the plate on an upturned milk crate. I reached for one politely, and bit down. My jaw nearly locked. I pretended to chew. "Umm."

Behind Mrs. G, Grady Thumbs held his belly, laughing silently. He shifted his eyes to the railing giving me the go-ahead, so when Ida turned to reach for her drink, I gave the cookie a flip with my wrist and sent the rock to cookie heaven. I brushed my hands together and swallowed loudly.

"We didn't have a chance to talk much at the pool," Ida was saying. "Do you have children?"

"Yes, one daughter. She's in Belize doing missionary work with her husband."

"Oh, how exciting, I'm sure. Still, they do have the malaria there and probably some other flesh-eating diseases. Is she taking vitamins?"

"Her husband is a doctor, so I'm sure they've taken precautions." I felt Grady push something cold into my hand. Heineken. I could hear my church choir clucking their tongues. *Oh, May. You've really fallen to a new low, haven't you?* Grady leaned discreetly to the side, and a brief unpleasant smell drifted by on a subtle breeze.

"Scuz me," he said, and then belched. "Doctor huh? Nice. What about you? Your husband is…"

"Deceased," I said, quickly and easily. I had prepared myself for this. "Five years." Don't know where that came from though, it just seemed like a nice, round figure. He liked round figures. That thought came to mind out of nowhere, and I was afraid for a minute I'd spoken out loud. But the two nodded in understanding, so I relaxed. The Heineken helped.

"My Joe has been gone for twelve years. Grady here has left a trail of broken hearts. Three wives, and how many children?"

"Five. Three girls, two boys, all doing fine."

I wanted to keep the focus away from me since I was unskilled at lying, so I chattered on. I was becoming a bit sleepy as the beer wormed its way through my varicose veins.

"What did you do, Grady?" A second beer found its way into my hand. Risky, but I wasn't ready to go home yet. I didn't know if Mrs. Berkowitz ever slept, but I was still holding onto the hope.

"This guy here was a banker," Ida interrupted. Grady seemed comfortable letting her talk for him. "I've seen his scrapbooks and photo albums. Looked dapper in his day. He was quite the businessman. But what about you? Did you work?"

"No, I took care of the house and my daughter. My husband was a doctor, too, and with all the social engagements, there wasn't much time for me to do much else. For a while I wanted to be a writer."

It seemed like a confession. I'd never told anyone before about my dream, and now that I'd mentioned it, I felt somehow obliged to do something about it.

"A writer, now that's something. If you get a few pages down, I'd be glad to look them over. You know, for grammar and whatnot." Mrs. Gateway seemed genuinely eager. Then she frowned. "But not commas. I could never get the commas right."

"I'll do that," I promised, but thought of the computer and what I would do if I finally got one. This seemed an easy segue into dangerous territory. I had to know more about Mrs. Berkowitz. Armed with distilled courage, I took the plunge. Sadly, it made a splash that was about as cataclysmic as Joyce's cannonball.

"Mrs. Berkowitz has offered to help me learn how to use a computer."

The wind began to blow like God himself had let out a tremendous gasp. The cookie drops flipped upside down onto the floor of the balcony. Potted plants tumbled onto the lawn below. The sky lit up in a rocket burst of lightning, followed soon after by a thunderous crash. Mrs. Gateway and Mr. Thumbs were caught in a still-life photo, and a train took that moment to blast by the apartment complex, laying heavily on its horn.

"That was close," Grady said. I think he was referring to the lightning, but I wasn't sure. There was more to that statement than a mere comment about the weather.

"We'd better get inside." Ida hurried in a nervous pace, collecting bottles, gathering what hadn't been skittered about by the wind.

"Rain's coming for sure." Grady stuck his fingers into the empties, shouldering his way through the balcony door.

I'd managed to bust up another party. Darn.

"What a minute. What's with everyone? I say the old lady's name, and people act like I've yelled fire in a theater." I stood in the doorway, shouting above the din. My lips felt a little rubbery, my knees a little wobbly, but gosh darn it, all this secretive, dismissive stuff had to end. I wanted answers. I wanted *data*.

"Come in and close the door, May, you're getting wet." Mrs. G. sounded tired, like someone who had fought the good fight, but she was finally throwing in the towel.

Another crash of thunder pushed me through the door. I closed it in a hurry. Grady glanced from me to Ida, looking like a boy waiting for permission from his mother to speak.

"Let me get us some coffee, then we'll have a little chat. I suppose it's time you knew." Grady seemed relieved that Mrs. G had taken the initiative. His white hair was in a mess on his head. He absently combed through it with restless fingers. He found a place on the couch and sat with his elbows on his thighs. His black eyebrows danced, his eyes darted about, and he cleared his throat enough times to be distracting.

"Now, we're getting somewhere," I said. Where had that woman come from? Who was I to speak so boldly? It just came out, bubbling up from the rigid control I'd maintained, wondering what in the world could make them so nervous. I wandered about, waiting for Ida's return. A collection of photos on the wall held my attention for the duration. Generations of Gateways smiled at me.

"It's decaf. Hope that's okay." Ida was back with a tray of steaming mugs. I took one. Now. The moment of truth. "You take the rocker." Ida nodded toward a stout wooden chair, so I sat on its edge, looking and waiting, slurping and trying not to make a face. The coffee was bad. Really bad.

"She's not a nice woman," Ida said. "There's things about her... Things you shouldn't know."

"I can hardly see how I can keep from finding out. After all, I live right across from her."

"She'll get under your skin if you let her," Ida said.

I thought of the songs, the strange questions, the things she knew about me. It must have shown.

"She already knows," Grady said to Ida while studying my face. His skin was ashen; crimson streaks colored the hollows of his cheeks. He didn't look well.

"*What* do I know?" I leaned forward, nearly toppling the rocker, splashing the coffee.

"Does she talk to you about things nobody else could know but you?" Mrs. G asked.

"Has she written you any letters or sent you any packages? That sort of thing?" Grady asked.

"Have you caught her with your mail? Has she ever answered your phone?" Mrs. G. was breathing fast. Her face was pinched, like she'd been pinched.

"My phone? No! She's never even been in my apartment!"

"And she's never done anything, well, out of the ordinary?"

I wanted to tell them about the question, *Why didn't you kick him out?* I wanted to tell them about my husband, what had happened, why I was here, and why I'd left a house with eight bedrooms, five bathrooms and a heated pool next to a greenhouse, and why I was driving a vintage Camaro with license plates that said STUD DOC. But I couldn't. I was embarrassed, and I wanted to hold onto my privacy. I didn't know these people. They were probably as nutty as everyone else in this place, and I was only there *temporarily*. I shook my head, mustering a look of shocked disbelief. They bought it.

Mrs. Gateway started breathing normally; Mr. Thumbs stuck one of his in the air and fell back against the cushions.

"Okay, then." Grady chuckled, but it was forced. "Don't worry about a thing, then."

Don't worry about a thing, then? On my way back to my apartment that was all I could do. Worry, and wonder about Mrs. Berkowitz. Tomorrow I was going back to the computer store, and by nightfall I would pay Mrs. B. another visit, come hell or fake hairdo.

SIX

"MAY BELL LIST! Buenos Dias, Missy List!"

The next day I woke up with a mouth full of cotton balls and a head full of spiky cobwebs. It had been years since my last hangover, a hard lesson then, and the best reason now, to keep beer bottles from darkening my lips in the future.

I looked at my clock. Two ones stood side by side. I groaned on my way to the door, wishing I had a Rottweiler.

"May Bell!" Through the peephole, two small, brown faces beamed with neighborly cheer. Mr. Ramirez showed off his polished tooth.

What now?

I pushed the door open a crack, and winced when sunshine stuck daggered fingers through my eyeballs.

"Only thirty minutes until exercise class down at Senior Center. You don't want to miss it!"

"Exercise what?" I felt queasy. Go away.

"Aerobics. Great fun, you'll see!" Without giving me a chance to decline, the cheerful duo moved off down the stairs, swishing in their squint-green Lycra.

Great. The last thing I felt like doing was groove to

the oldies. Wait a minute; it might be a way for me to get closer to some of the residents. Inexperienced as I was at pumping the locals for information, it had to be done. My *gather data* page was only half filled.

Forget workout clothes; in the bottom of my closet I found a pair of too-tight gray sweat pants that, regrettably, drew screaming attention to my dimpled hams. That just couldn't be helped. Next problem was finding adequate bondage material for my fine mammary abundance. Sports bras weren't my style, but I did find one Playtex job, built as sturdy as an Egyptian pyramid, so I squeezed into that one.

And I saw that it was good.

I peeked to be sure I'd remembered some cotton panties for sweat absorption, just in case this exercise stuff was for real. A T-shirt topped it off.

On my way out, I checked the mirror. Egad. I hadn't taken off my makeup the night before, and black patches of mascara ran in smudges from my eyebags to my cheeks. I scrubbed up with a washcloth, combed water through my hair, scoured my teeth and checked the time. Five minutes. Forget breakfast; I'd just have to load up on a few Krispy Kremes when it was all over.

I closed the door to my apartment as softly as I could while keeping a nervous eye on apartment 3C. Halfway down the stairs I heard her.

"I'm just a luv machine, and I don't work for nobody but you, oooh baby, a love and kiss machine, come on over here, let me give it to you."

Neighbor Ratchet was singing softly; "machine" came out like *mutcheen*. I halted, my foot held aloft. It was the song I'd heard my husband purr over the phone one evening.

It had been the *coup de grace,* the last straw, the clincher, as my mom would say. My husband was crooning on the phone in our den, his back to the door. He thought I was sleeping, I thought he was reading. I just wanted to bring him a glass of milk, but I'd caught him. He hadn't heard me come in, but I'd sure as heck heard him singing to Bambie, or Tasha, or whoever, and I started packing the next day.

This had to be just stupid, simple coincidence. Lots of people knew that song. It didn't mean anything at all. Nothing at all.

I whirled around, searching her apartment anxiously, expecting to catch her bald little head poking through the door. A shadow passed behind the balcony screen like a fluttering bird. There was no more singing, causing me to question whether or not I'd actually heard her after all. I tripped down the remaining steps, my nerves all a-jingle.

"Does she talk to you about things nobody else could know but you?"

"Has she written you any letters, or sent you any packages, that sort of thing?"

"Have you caught her with your mail? Has she ever answered your phone?"

"She's never done anything, well, out of the ordinary?"

Everything was out of the ordinary, and *everyone* was out of the ordinary. There wasn't anything I wanted more than to catch the first Greyhound back home, or to Belize, or to any place that was familiar, warm and comfortable. There was just one thing that kept me from bolting like a scared rabbit. I had to find out more about Mrs. Berkowitz. I had to have some answers to this crazy mixed-up puzzle. My whole adult life I'd spent running from things, pretending everything was okay when it wasn't. I was a new May Bell, determined to find strength from somewhere. First, though, May Bell had an appointment with some dumbbells, or barbells, or hell's bells.

The Senior Center, that lively come-greet-your-neighbors hub of activity, was all abuzz with blue hairs and leotards. It made a person imagine what these bodies had been when their atrophied muscles were at full hormone levels, and when dem bones weren't osteoporosis-opposed. Chairs were pushed against walls; tables were folded and stacked atop a blonde, polished wood floor. Everyone was forming lines, their jiggly arms extending everywhere, selfishly marking territory.

I heard turmoil from the back of the pack and didn't even have to look. I was becoming accustomed to the sounds Mr. Bob What-What made at the commencement of his appearances.

And here he came.

Decked out in control-top panty hose (with built-in

panty, thank the stars), squeezed at the top by a crino-
line tutu, Bob's hairy chest and naked bulging belly
came forth, but I scarcely had time to consider this a
distraction. He silenced us all with a leap that would
make a Lipizaner proud, fell back to earth deftly on his
toes, did a fine pirouette, and ran in tiny steps toward
the front of the room. He did another graceful leap,
even higher than the one before. His arms were out,
fingers splayed and back, fleshy chin thrust toward
the ceiling. For a moment he took a position of calm
meditation, eyes closed.

Quick adjustment. Bob bent low, and erupted into
a rapid tap number. Shuffle, ball, change, shuffle, ball,
change. His arms criss-crossed crazily in front of his
groin. This brought resounding applause.

"Excuse me, excuse me." April Fleet flung residents left and right on her way to Mr. What-What.
As she passed a buzzing fan, her skirt whipped up,
giving us all a look at her control tops (without the
panties built in).

"What? What?" Bob insisted while April prodded
him forward and out the door. The lines formed anew.
Colorful ribbons of purples and turquoise, and fluores-
cent greens. There I was, looking very much the
newcomer in my gray cotton sweats and T, when off
to my left I heard a metallic clatter. A woman of about
a hundred shuffled along, bent crookedly over a silver
walker. She thudded to a halt next to my thigh, and
twisted her neck to look at me.

"Haven't missed a-one of these in three years," she said.

"That's nice," I answered. How in the world she was going to manage around that aluminum partition I didn't have a clue, but I knew my face didn't show my concern because, after all, I'd been brought up proper.

A deafening shriek came from the platform in the front, and my head shot up to focus on a woman of about fifty, prancing about in a bright pink spandex affair. Around her neck hung a long, braided cord, dangling a silver umpire's whistle, the source of the noise. Her legs were long and lean, her hair was in a ponytail, (ridiculous to have long hair after forty, my mother used to say, not dignified), and the skin on her arms and shoulders was a leathery brown. She probably plays five games of tennis before breakfast. That'll give her cancer before she's fifty-five. The doctor will be scraping blotchy patches off her back with a scalpel, but she'll think it's nothing and go another round just to prove it. Dead by sixty.

"All right kids! Time to stretch!"

Kids? Who was she fooling? Everyone around me seemed to know the drill. Men and women were bending side-to-side, arms held overhead. Lots of groaning and moaning, and the inevitable gunshots from calcified joints when the more adventurous sorts did deep knee bends. The old lady on my left clung to her walker, squatting like she was doing a *plie* at the bar. She was already panting.

"I'm Fanny Piller. Haven't seen you here before," she said.

Piller. Sounded like pillow with a Southern accent. Fanny. Funny, because she didn't have one. She was as withered, wrinkled, and compressed as a summer grape. On the back of her head waved a single, pink, cushy curler—either she'd missed that one or it was on purpose, or maybe she'd started something then forgot what she was doing in the middle of it.

"Ain't you that nurse I had in '52?"

"No, no, I think you must be mistaken."

Fanny looked over her brackets and squinted behind glasses so thick that they made her eyes seem grossly over-proportioned.

"Yes, you're right. She was a Negro lady. What was her name?"

Fanny was lost somewhere in '52 and the acrobat at the front of the class was demonstrating her agility. She threw a long leg up to her shoulder and gave a mighty kick. I was hoping that wasn't expected of me. I had given up on any promise that Fanny would be helpful in the data department, so I shuffled away, bending and swaying, jockeying myself between two writhing gentlemen.

"Spent four months in the bush," one of the men said. He scissored his hands, cutting the air in front of my face. "I could make a man dead without ever leaving a mark."

"Then this should be child's play," I faltered. I

glanced longingly back at Fanny. Maybe I shouldn't have pressed my luck.

"Probably didn't serve a day in his life." The man to my right was dangling his hands by his knees in a configuration that said he wouldn't be able to right himself without the aid of paramedics. I was wrong. He stood up, tall and lanky, his face burning crimson. "Watch that he don't bop you in the nose. Delusions mixed with Parkinson's. Not exactly a friendly combo."

I smiled weakly and once again focused on the platform. Miss Feel-The-Burn was tweeting that irritating whistle again. I guessed the stretching part was over.

"Now. Everyone limbered up? Goood." The music started, some Big Band arrangement, evidently giving her the desire to kick up that flippety leg of hers again.

"Everyone, knee up!"

It looked like Lord Help Us of the Dance. Hands were waving, knees were rising, but none too high; the eucalyptus gels were heating up.

"Keep to the beat now."

Grunts. Lots of grunts, and I think Fanny was beginning to swoon but I didn't care to look. "Now, everyone jump!"

Jump?

I was in a pack of lemmings with little else to do but follow along. My feet pushed away from the hardwood floor and I was sailing higher than anyone in the room. I wanted Miss No-Pain-No-Gain to see me defy gravity, to see me reach for the fluorescents, to see me punching my fists skyward.

I came back to earth hard. It was a ripple effect, really. First my feet hit, and then my thighs rushed down, followed by my ample rear end, slamming the tops of my hamstrings. Finally, the pendulums, in what I regretfully discovered were unfettered in their not too supportive bra, nearly pulled me the rest of the way to the floor.

"Again!"

Again? Not on your life.

SEVEN

MY APARTMENT FELT cool after the Senior Center Sweatshop. I was disappointed. I'd only made contact with three people at the pummel convention: Mr. Scissorhands, Mr. Lanky, and Fanny. No info there. As I peeled off my sweat pants, I wondered how and when I had allowed myself to get so out of shape.

After a vat of rum raisin ice cream, I showered and got into my car, on my way to the computer store. There were stories to write, tomes to type, letters to send, not to mention a good excuse to find a way back in to see Mrs. Berkowitz.

I spied Mr. Greenjeans while backing out of the carport. He knelt behind a hedge and peered around it, holding a trowel in his hand. There was a mound of dirt by his knees where he'd been digging. Maybe he was digging up that dead mouse.

The computer store was just as I'd left it.

"So. You decided?"

The pierced boy popped up from behind a stack of boxes. He had a new staple in his lower lip, tempting me to call him Lance. It seemed fitting.

"I need a PC. One with a lot of hard drive." I'd learned a little something. Take that Mr. Lance.

"Okay," he said slowly. "A lot of hard drive? You need a lot of memory?"

"My memory is just fine. I recognize *you,* don't I?" Lance was making me uneasy again, and he'd just insulted my memory. I'd like to give *him* a scissor.

Lance just lifted his eyebrow ring and motioned me to follow. He was sighing again.

"This should do you. Plenty of hard drive." Sigh. Sigh.

"Good. I'll need someone to take this to my car."

"Do you have a mouse?"

The image of Greenjeans passed through my mind. "Whatever makes it go."

"Keyboard?"

"I just keep mine in my purse." I shook my handbag. House keys and car keys made a satisfying jingle.

Sigh, sigh, "I'll set you up. Just wait by the cash register."

"Fine." Head held high, I was finally a member of the new millennium. He was going to *set me up.* That's what Mrs. Berkowitz had said; her son had *set her up.* Excitement about it all made me eager to get the thing whirring and blinking. Move over Melville.

I didn't even take a Starbucks detour on my way back to the complex.

The darn thing was in the trunk of my car. I stood staring at STUD DOC, not knowing how in heaven's name I was going to lug the boxes up the stairs to my apartment. Mr. Greenjeans was nowhere in sight, but I could hear the mariachi music moaning clear as day. I walked over to the Ramirez balcony and leaned over the railing to give a shout. Paco stared up at me, all ears and eyeballs. Yap, yap, yap.

"Hello?" I squinted at the screen door looking for signs of life. I knew Mr. Ramirez was in there, because I could see his shadow; at least I thought it was his shadow, it was hard to tell.

"Mr. Ramirez?" Someone turned down the music. I wanted to turn down Paco. Yap, yap, yap.

"May List!" Mr. and Mrs. Ramirez appeared in the porch doorway and shoved the screen aside. Were they attached at the hip?

"I have more tamales, jus' you wait. I get them for you." Mrs. Ramirez slid back behind the door. So, they weren't attached.

I took the drooling package, ignored the dog yap, and asked Mr. Ramirez for a favor. I needed help carrying the boxes, and would he be so kind?

It took a bit of struggling, but we got them into my apartment, ripped off the tape, and before long had cardboard and packaging material littering the floor. Mr. Mariachi had smiled throughout the whole ordeal, his gold tooth leading the way. Tiny beads of sweat sprouted on the bridge of his nose, so I offered a Coke from the fridge to be polite, but he waved me off. Nice little man.

"I noticed your writer machine was broken. I borrowed some of the pieces, hope you don't mind."

"You took my typewriter?"

Mr. Ramirez looked ashamed. "Just the pieces that fell off. I like to build things with whatever I can find. Was that okay?"

I lifted a hand. "I was going to get rid of it anyway," I lied. I was getting pretty good at it lately. Being brought up proper, I didn't want him to feel bad.

"That's why I got this computer. It will make life so much easier."

"It's too hot up here though; you'll need to get some fans because electronics don't like too much heat. Makes 'em cranky."

"I know the feeling," I said under my breath. Mr. Mariachi had been helpful, but it was time for him to go. He was lingering, for whatever reason, and I was running out of things to talk about.

Mr. Ramirez looked around the apartment, swabbed his neck with a handkerchief, and plucked at his shirt. "It's better downstairs. Anita can cook all day and it's still cool."

Yeah, I thought, because all of the heat comes up here. The smell of tamales was back, drifting from the place by the sink. Another trip to the Dumpster was in order.

"Thank you Mr. Ramirez. Thank you so much." I was edging toward the door, impatient to take a look at my new equipment without the embarrassment of someone watching me fumble through the setup, but he just stood assessing things while mopping away.

"You know how to use this stuff?" He pointed a golden tooth at the boxes.

"Not yet, not really, but Mrs. Berkowitz has offered to help me."

The hanky stopped. The tooth vanished behind a frowning lip. "She can't help. Best stay clear Missy List; really, it's for the best."

There it was again. The warning, the mood shift, the nervous look.

"What? What?" Mr. Bob shouted out from downstairs. Gold tooth grinned widely, and huh, huhed, and then stuffed the hanky in his back pocket.

"I'd better go rescue Anita. He's loose again."

Mr. Ramirez scooted out the door, leaving me with the feeling that I'd just eaten something from the wrong end of the cow. I shook off his warning. Tonight I would try again. I was getting close—I could feel it. I hoped, though, that I wasn't planning something daring like stopping a fan blade with my tongue. Speaking of fans, I had to go get those box fans. It was closing in on three hundred degrees and I didn't want a cranky computer to deal with. Time to take another cruise.

I popped in a tape once I got the car rolling. Tina Turner. "What's Love Got to Do with It?" Sing it Tina. Take that Ike. Take that STUD DOC. First though, there on the corner was the green Starbucks sign. The fans could wait.

"Hey Lady, nice car." A kid with jeans sagging below his waistline traced the lines of the Camaro. He had his arm crooked around the neck of his girlfriend, who looked as if she were dead from the shoulders up. "'67?"

"'68. Herst shifter, three-speed on the floor, 327 under the hood." Ted wasn't the only one who appreciated a fine piece of tin. Too bad he didn't have the same taste in classic women. His loss.

I left the gawking couple and swung through the door into the intoxicating smell of fresh coffee. What will it be today? I glanced over the menu high on the wall, settling on my usual. Just couldn't get enough brain pain. The perky girl packed it to go, and soon I was on my way to Target, picked up a couple of box fans because it was all I could carry, and headed home.

Cool for once, errands completed, I was feeling close to normal. Tina sang, "I'm Your Private Dancer," reminding me of my STUD DOC and his private dancers. Had it been his idea to let Mrs. Berkowitz in on our private little life? The more I turned it over, the less sense it made. People were afraid of her. It was untenable to think Ted could have gotten to everyone, so I decided to let it go. It wouldn't be long before I was far and away from that place, so what did I care?

Let it go? Before the next stop sign I was again trying to figure out a new way to solve the mystery of crazy old Mrs. Berkowitz.

Thinking hard, I wasn't paying close attention to the traffic in front of me until I noticed brake lights. May, the human projectile. Almost. At the end of my sliding stop, I saw the woman in the Taurus I'd nearly kissed with my front bumper. She was shock white, crossing herself, glaring at me in her mirror. At least she didn't give me the finger.

I didn't feel like waiting in traffic. There were flashing lights ahead and it looked like I'd be sitting there awhile, so I pulled out of traffic and into a nearby parking lot, grabbed my Frappuccino and went walking.

Out of the cement and sound barriers rose an entrance to a lovely park with gravel trails in and around pudgy bushes. I perused the view as my feet crunched steadily along. When was the last time I'd taken a walk? People were smiling, walking dogs there, tossing Frisbees here, having picnics, and smoking cigarettes. Normal people. A woman pushed a stroller. She waved. I waved back. Walk, walk, my muscles relaxed. It felt so good I must have walked for two hours, and by the time my blistered feet said it was time to quit, I was soaked through. This should be a routine—something to do every day. I'd add it to my list. Goodbye to the old May Bell, hello to the new. Maybe I could manage another one of those exercise classes after all.

I got back to the insane asylum just in time to catch Mr. Greenjeans hanging over the lip of the carport roof. He had nails in his mouth, and a hammer under his arm, so I assumed he had business up there. I hoisted the fans, one per hip, and struggled across the parking lot toward my stairwell. If I looked at the ground as I walked, maybe the active seniors would take a hint and leave me alone. I wasn't so lucky.

"Missy List! Do you need a hand?"

It was Mr. Ramirez, talking loudly over Paco, who peered through the slats in the balcony wall barking Chihuahua insults. I wanted to give the yapper a poke in those beady eyes, but both of my hands were occupied.

I shook my head no thanks and prayed he would hush. I didn't want to alert Mrs. Berkowitz just yet. She was still in her apartment, had in fact never left her apartment that I could remember, and I wasn't prepared for any more surprises. Playing hide and seek when I was a kid was fun, as long as I was the one jumping out from behind trees to say, "You're it!" I didn't like it when the game went the other way. Some things never change.

"Alrighty then. Anita will bring up something later if you'd like." Smiling, smiling, Paco yap, yap, yapping.

"That would be nice." I lied. One more tamale parcel and I might be forced to eat one. "Just leave it at the door, please. I'm going to take a little nap." Another lie. I wanted to do some more thinking and I didn't want to be disturbed.

The fans were soon buzzing at the foot of my bed. I went to my refrigerator to begin a purging event to equal no other. Out went the rum raisin, the Peachy Keen vanilla, and Choco-Chocolate, down the drain with a squirt of the sink hose. Oreos, Nutter Butters, Doritos and Fritos landed in the trashcan with a sad but satisfying crunch. Then I took a cleansing breath before placing both feet on the bathroom scale. Yikes. So many numbers. Never mind, this was the jumping-off place. Even so, Milk Duds would have eased the pain.

I sat on my bed in the comfort of the fan wind, holding pen and paper. It took some shifting and adjusting before I could write without the papers fluttering. I wrote:

Eat only healthy foods

Diet

Exercise

Ask Mrs. Berkowitz to teach me about computers.

I paused at the last one. Tonight? Best to keep it after hours when the neighbors wouldn't be so prone to talk. Tonight it would be. Check the time. Still early enough for a swim in the pool, if I could make it without alerting my cellmates.

A paisley tan bathing suit contained most of what I wanted hidden, but I grabbed a giant towel anyway, and swaddled everything else that I wanted to veil, which included just about every part of my body, except my feet and hands. At what point does one stop caring?

It was my husband. He always made me feel ashamed of the way I looked. Ashamed and embarrassed, comparing me to the other, younger, women at the country club. Well, he wasn't going to be waiting by the pool ogling the anorexic top-heavy cocktail waitresses, so who was I trying to impress? This was the dawning of a new day. Or the dawning of a new May. Private dancer indeed. I grabbed the towel in defiance and swung it over my shoulder. Just in case, though, I donned sunglasses as I headed out.

My flip-flops slapped along the sidewalk like laughing applause. I drew near the pool gate, using all of my reserve to keep the towel resting over my shoulder. I sucked it all in, but my stomach muscles had forgotten years ago how to concave.

Little ponds of nervous sweat were already beginning to gather in that valley that looked more like a long wrinkle than cleavage. At least the mounds were above my navel.

I thought of a joke I'd once heard.

"Doctor, there's an elderly woman here with a gunshot to the knee."

"How'd it happen?"

"She was trying to commit suicide."

"I don't get it."

"She heard it would be fatal if she shot herself just below the left breast."

I looked around for a chair and noted the familiar faces. Mr. Scissorhands was across the way, demonstrating a chokehold on someone I didn't recognize. It didn't look serious. Mr. Greenjeans was wandering around, scooping stuff from the water with a big net on a long pole. Fanny was sitting in the shallow end; all but her tiny shoulders and head were immersed in the clear water. She wasn't wearing her glasses, and much to my astonishment, her eyes were just as huge without them. I noticed something silver and metallic at her feet. It was her walker, poised and ready for use, at the bottom of the pool. Did she swim with the thing, thumping along, her shriveled feet kicking and flicking behind her?

Bob What-What was actually in a bathing suit—a small black Speedo—although it was on backward, which made a strange vision when he turned around to adjust the towel in his lounge chair. The Mariachis had made their way down and were fussing over an odorous hibachi. The plant man was dipping a cup in the pool and went about watering all of the decorative plastic ferns. I decided then his name, until I knew it, would be Fernon. No wonder the plants had an odd albino look around the bottom leaves—chlorine and chemicals would do that. No accounting for the odd albino looks of the creased faces peering at me from under fat brimmed hats. From the neck down, there was pink frosting on some, where they had been too chintzy with the lotion.

"Watch this, May!" I squinted up at the head of the pool where Grady was waving wildly. He stood on a diving board, which, by the way, was only about a foot above the deep end, which, by the way, plunged all the way to a mere six feet. *NO DIVING!* said one of the precautionary signs posted on the chain link. What in the world were you supposed to do with the diving board then?

Grady bounced once, twice, three times, got a little air between his toes and the bobbing board, and flung himself out toward the sea, grasped his knees and hit the water. Squeals and confusion from the coffee

klatch, and women were raising fists even before
Thumbs broke the surface. The gaggle of old women
were rescuing their totes, and wringing their towels,
officially ending their poolside card game.

I scooted a lounge chair over to the shade. It had
white plastic webbing, the kind that left an impression
no matter how you sat on it, and smoothed my towel.
Grady emerged, his white hair streaming, and pushed
himself up to a sitting position on the edge of the pool.
His trunks made a squelching, embarrassing, kissing
sound when he twisted and plopped.

"May Bell!" He shaded his eyes. I waited for the
thumbs-up sign; yep, there it was, just a single this time.
The front of his trunks had taken air, forming bubbles
on top of his thighs. While his legs were a bit on the thin
side, they weren't half bad really. I could imagine he'd
been an athlete sometime in his life. There was still an
indication of ribbony muscles under the gauzy skin. He
smoothed his hair back, a full head of it, white and
thick, an unusual contrast to his dark eyebrows. When
he smiled there was an attractive Borgnine gap between
his front teeth. Why was I noticing such things? It wasn't
as if I was meeting him for the first time, but there was
a little distance between us, and I felt at ease making
note. That was something I'd have to learn if I was going
to be a real writer. Notice the details and store them for
later use. *Gather data.* Oh brother. He was coming over.
His sidekick, Ida Gateway, was nowhere in sight, so I
would have to make conversation on my own.

"I'm going for a Coke. Can I get you one?" Thumbs grabbed a towel on the way over, patted his face, and then dropped the soggy lump on the chair beside mine. I suppose that meant he would be staying a while. He didn't wait for a reply, just gave a wink and was gone. I could hear coins plunking into the machine nearby. Where had he been hiding the change? Back in a flash, he had two sweating cans of Coke. I took one gratefully. It was getting warmer by the second; however, I'd just gotten into a position where most of my better features were just so. I'd have to put up with some minor discomfort if I didn't want to expose my waffle imprints by moving over to the inviting poolside.

"Ida and I are getting together again this evening. Want to come by for a visit?" Grady was slurping at his drink, sitting on the side of the lounge chair, nonplussed that his shorts were riding high on one side. I kept my attention focused on his eyebrows. I mentally went over the litany of excuses and dismissed them one by one, since, alas, there were no social events to plan, no dinners to prep for, no waiting husband. There was Mrs. Berkowitz to think about; although it wasn't a factor I would throw out just yet.

"That sounds fine," I surrendered, and then popped the Coke tab, angry at my weakness. I could have just said no.

"Heard anything from that daughter of yours in Brazil? What's she doing again? Studying the apes?"

"Medical mission work. In Belize. And no, I haven't."

Thumbs grinned and tried to stifle a burp. He thumped his chest. "I knew that. Just wanted to see if you were paying attention. You look miles away."

"Wish I were." Had I really said that? Grady looked at me with a knowing expression. So, I had really said it. The statement had been true enough; even so, I wanted to take it back. The last thing I wanted was sympathy from a horny man I barely knew.

He surprised me by touching my arm. "Then why don't you go?" It was more a statement than a question. Maybe I had insulted him. No, his eyes weren't hard.

"I can't." I thought of the conversation with the apartment manager, the broken lease and the money down the drain, not to mention the trouble I'd had finding the apartment in the first place. My back was sore just thinking about moving all of those boxes again. More than that, I didn't want to admit that I was a failure at being liberated. I had my pride.

"She's gotten to you then." Grady pushed air out through his teeth and his dark eyebrows furrowed. "Damn!" He leaned back in the chair and gazed out over the pool, his face set in a look of frustration.

"What are you talking about?" I lowered my voice; it just seemed the right thing to do.

"That old hag. She does it sooner or later. And once she's in, you can't get her out. Don't even try. We've all tried."

"I really don't know what you mean. Who?" I waited again, not for the thumbs-up but for the name.

I could see it floating above his head just waiting for it to come down and fall from his mouth.

"Mrs. Berkowitz."

Thunk. Like a dart hitting the bull's eye. I still didn't know what Grady was talking about, exactly, but my curious nature was buzzing, so I pretended like I understood, if nothing else but to keep him talking. Nod, nod, yes, I certainly agree. He glanced around the slow moving crowd of human seals; no need to worry, they were all caught up in their own activities of exchanging recipes or lathering up. There was even one woman knitting under a big umbrella.

"*What* do I know?" This was an open-ended question, aimed at drawing him out a bit more. I was getting tired of talking in code. Let's cut to the chase. When had I started thinking like this? Must be the books I was reading. A bit too much Cornwell. Chink, chink, chink. A metallic clatter broke up the mood. Fanny was finished with her aquatic gymnastics and shuffled past, bent over the walker with the determination of a triathlete heading for the finish line.

"'Jeopardy' in fifteen minutes," she said to her watch.

"Hello Fanny," Grady said.

"'Jeopardy' in fifteen minutes."

"Hi Fanny," I said.

"'Jeopardy' in fifteen minutes. Or was that 'Dragnet'? 'Jeopardy'? Oh frazzle. I think I missed 'Judge Judy.'" Chink, chink, chink. Out the gate and away she went, her tiny feet gathering speed.

The clatter of her walker had barely diminished when Bob passed us. The backwards Speedo must have been uncomfortable but the wedgie didn't slow him down. Grady chuckled, I blew on my sunglasses. "Come on over for a Heine later. We'll talk then." Thumbs squelched out of the seat and put out his hand. I took it, thanked him politely, and stood beside the chair.

"Around eight?" I asked.

"Make it nine. 'Jeopardy' is on in fifteen minutes." I waited until he was out of sight and grabbed up my towel, then raced back to my apartment. Not much time. I had to talk to Mrs. Berkowitz.

EIGHT

MY FLIP-FLOPS clopped along the sidewalk, startling Mr. Greenjeans as I rounded the corner to my apartment. He'd left his pool duties to putter, now caulking the outer edge of Bob's window, and I could hear the muted, "What? What?" from the other side of the glass. Bob's round face peered through an opening in the drapes. He was tracking the handyman and made little foggy clouds on the inside of the window with his mouth and nose. The Mariachis were probably having a siesta. Even Paco was silent, but a salsa band was moaning on as faithfully as ever. When I got to the top of the stairs, I noticed Anita had placed a new foil-wrapped package near my door. I carried it in, waiting for the smell to slam my sinuses, but this time when I peeled away the edges I was happy to find brownies. They got close to my lips before my new life's resolution waved its red banner. *What about those thighs, May Bell? This ain't gonna look good at the pool tomorrow. Wanta waste that jog around the park?* I wanted to curse more than ever, but I didn't. The brownie went back in with its family and I sealed the deal. Then a thought struck me. *Have a brownie Mrs. Berkowitz, just being neighborly and all. Have another. Have the whole darn bunch. And while you gobble, I just have a few questions I'd like to ask.*

Off came the bathing suit and into the shower I went. Man! It was hot. So much for nerves of steel. What was it about this old woman that made my stomach turn to jelly? Not just the outside, but the inside too, and all of my newfound muscles. All jelly and wiggling around with no place to settle. Later, I stood in front of the mirror using my hair dryer as a defogger. Juggling a bit, I drew some lipstick around, combed my hair neatly, and smoothed down my dress. Not bad.

As I walked through the living room, it was as if I was moving through a long corridor extending out and out into a black hole, a narrow dark passage with no end in sight. My floor felt like I was on a small boat—shifting and swaying. I moved through a river of thick, muddy fear. Slowly, slowly.

This was ridiculous. Come on May. I scooped up the foil package and marched to the door. I turned the knob. Breathe May, breathe. She was standing in front of me even before I knocked.

"Ready for that answer now Maybe Baby?" I wanted to bop her and run. I did neither.

"I got a new computer. I was hoping you could help me." Breathe.

"Right this way!" She opened the door wide. "You're just in time for tea."

"I brought some brownies." It didn't matter; she was pulling me in by the wrist.

"Can't have one now, blood sugar level is a bit high. Just leave them on the coffee table, never turned down a brownie in my life." Mrs. Berkowitz had a new look. She was now a redhead, with braids no less, sprouting out from just above her ears. Her lobes were stretched nearly to her shoulders by the weight of industrial-sized hoop earrings. The Pippi Gabore look. Nice. She was wearing black Capri pants and a heavy sweater. Make that the Pippi Gabore Petrie look. Didn't she know we were having a heat wave? On the other hand, her apartment was comfortably cool, even chilly. Nevertheless, I was beginning to dribble down my front. I blotted.

Fidgeting, I looked around the apartment, finding new things. There was an exquisitely carved German cuckoo clock on the wall opposite the upside-down pictures. It ticked away the seconds, growing louder as I sat watching the little scuba diver in the bubbling, fishless aquarium.

"So how's that girl of yours in Belize? Found a cure for cancer yet?" Thud. I left a little more shin skin under the coffee table. I waited through the delay, waited, and then embraced the pain, smiling the whole time. "I guess not, we'd've heard about that on the news." She placed the chipped teacup in front of me and waved her hand over it.

"You know about my daughter?" I asked calmly. Steady, May Bell.

She didn't say anything, just squinted through the steam swirling from her cup and drew in the tea. It was so interesting how she could get her upper lip to dip so far down into the cup.

"Come on. Let's get started," she said abruptly.

"I really don't know anything about computers at all. Please make it simple."

"Come on, Maybe Baby, you're sitting there like a statue." Mrs. B. pointed toward her computer center. My legs moved, independent of conscious thought, carrying me forward. Her claws rested on my shoulders, pushing me into the chair. The doorbell rang and I nearly jumped out of my skin.

"I think someone is at the door."

Mrs. Berkowitz screeched with laughter, something I thought I'd gotten used to, but I jumped again, bouncing the keyboard. "That's my cuckoo clock, dizzy! I had it rigged that way. You know we don't have doorbells."

"Of course. The clock. How could I have been so silly?" A clock that sounded like a doorbell? What was the point? "See those little square things by your hand? Those are diskettes. I use CDs now, but for you, we'll start you on diskettes. They're like notebooks. They hold all sorts of information, you just slip them into the little space on the hard drive and…"

She went through the process, and I had it mastered after an hour. I was retrieving information, learning how to use the Word features, and had as much as I could handle when she exhaled noisily, and clapped her hands together.

"That's all for one day. You just take those empty disks and start on your book now. Didn't I tell you this was much better than that crazy old typewriter?"

I had to admit the computer age was all that it was cracked up to be.

"Now Mayfly," Mrs. Berkowitz grasped the chair and swung it around. My legs flew out from under the desk nearly grazing my shins one last time. She had me positioned directly in front of her; nothing I could do but stare into her leaky blue eyes, her face nearly touching mine. "You know condoms have been known to leak, especially with a few pin pricks, and I hear doctors make a load of money, especially when they're sued for adultery. What are you waiting for?"

"Why do you know all of this? Why are you talking like this?"

"Because you're a stupid woman. I'm surprised you don't have the imprints of his boot heels all over your back. Wait. Maybe you do. Let's take a look."

She reached for the collar of my dress and this time I really did scream. "Thank you for your time. Now I'm going to get out of here." I had a handful of diskettes, grabbed at my purse, threw my body into reverse, and raced from her apartment, afraid of my response if she'd really tried to rip off my dress. I didn't know how to do the scissor, but I could use a handy vase if need be. Her cackles followed me the rest of the way home.

I WAS A PRISONER in my own apartment. I didn't want to leave; no that's not true, I wanted to go, but didn't want to run into Mrs. Berkowitz on the way out. I fully expected Rod Serling to walk out of my bathroom fiddling with his zipper. A radio was what I needed. A little Rush Limbaugh, some Dr. Laura, or maybe a few Anne Murray tunes. Anything to bring the world back around to normal chaos. I stared at the phone. All I had to do was call the hospital, ask for Dr. List, eat crow and go home. The divorce wasn't final; I could keep my mouth shut, go back to life as usual, and be a stupid girl. *Dr. List? Oh yes, he's in surgery at the moment, at least I think that's what he said, some kind of operation. Giggle. He sure knows his anatomy!* Giggle. Best hands in the business! Giggle. And great with the instruments! Gag. Hang on, Maybe Baby; hold on now, the storm will pass.

I made good use of some nervous energy and tore through the computer boxes. I didn't have a suitable desk yet, so my miniature dining table would have to do. One thing about shock and fear: they either send you into a fugue state, or they sharpen the senses. I reserved my fugue state for later, and had the wires, cables, monitor and CPU together exactly as I remembered from looking at the info center across the way. It was humming before I gave into exhaustion. I wanted a nap, but the extra disks were at my elbow, and so I thumbed one in, watched the screen, and pulled up the menu. What I saw was nothing short of amazing. I had been expecting a blank screen where I would begin my novel, biography, poem, whatever struck my fancy, but instead, there was an extensive listing of names:

Abraham, Bradly Joe:

Adams, Janet:

Arnez, Phillip Sr.:

All in neat alphabetized rows, and all with their very own concise histories. I scanned pages and pages of details opposite coinciding names, and I must say, the facts following the names were not glowing. Janet Adams was listed as having cheated on her taxes, employed by Xerox for ten years, collected welfare checks. Phillip Arnez got a girl pregnant when he was sixteen, currently married with three daughters, living in Ft. Worth. Bradly Joe was booked twice for grand theft auto as a juvenile, currently working as a boat salesman in Portland, Oregon. The list went on. Not only were the names followed by less than shining biographies, but there were addresses, phone numbers, fax numbers, pager numbers, e-mail addresses, social security numbers, salary figures, you name it. A veritable Who's Who in human sludge.

I popped the diskette out of the port and turned it over in my hands. The plastic was worn and used, not like the shiny, new ones Mrs. Berkowitz had helped me with earlier. It was obvious I had picked up the wrong diskette by mistake in my rush to leave her little shop of horrors. A creeping sense of dread started at my feet and worked its way up to settle in the pooch of my stomach. Could there be? I shoved the diskette in again and scrolled down through the H file, past the I file, down, down to the J, K files and slowed at the L file. There it was. May Bell List. Big as life. The creeping sensation touched every fiber and nerve in my body. I was thankful to be sitting down, because I was sure at this point my legs wouldn't have supported me. Beside my name and all of the personal "who she is and how to find her" data was something that even my husband didn't know. *Married twice, first husband missing but not dead. Second marriage illegal.*

I pulled my hand away from the mouse as if I had been scorched. It couldn't be! My first husband had been killed in Korea. He and I had eloped a week before his reporting date, my parents didn't approve of him, and I never saw him after a tearful goodbye at the train station. We had planned to tell our families of our secret marriage after his return, but when the weeks turned into months with no word, then the months turned into years, it was assumed he had been killed in combat. His parents never gave up hope, but I guess no parent ever does. I got on with my life, and eventually married Ted. I'd buried the past. *Current marriage illegal.* Was it possible? I had never filed for a divorce from my first husband since I didn't think it was necessary. I had just gotten on with things.

The full impact of what that meant hit me like a thick board. That would make me a bigamist, and my daughter illegitimate! I had to get the diskette back to Mrs. Berkowitz. I couldn't let her know I had seen what terrible things she knew about other people, but how was I going to do that? Where did she get all of this? Why? How did she know? Thumbs knew. Mrs. Gateway knew. That's why they had been so afraid. That's what the warnings had been about.

I had been brought up proper; it's not nice to snoop, but morbid curiosity is a strong motivation. I scrolled through the list and it was no surprise when I found Ida Gateway's name. Her claim to fame was some sort of impropriety at the grade school back in '65. Grady Knox had been suspected of accepting and selling stolen property—tied to several nefarious characters. More and more names appeared in the inventory as my hunches were verified. Nearly every resident I had met at the Senior Center was mentioned with sins, big or small, following. There were hundreds of other names, people I didn't know, didn't care to know for that matter. Every variance of human malfeasance popped up before my eyes.

It was apparent I had just stepped into a den of lions. By chance or design, I had learned something about Mrs. Berkowitz, and what she had been doing in the dim light of night, but *where* she was getting this information was a mystery, and *why* was a greater mystery. I rubbed my hands together, noticed my palms were perspiring heavily, and hit the Save button. I'd get the diskette back, but not without keeping a little of the *data* for myself. When that was done, I pushed the button, and the diskette spit out of the computer mouth. I slipped it into my purse and pushed the Close button. Life at the Senior Center was getting increasingly more interesting.

NINE

I KEPT MY APPOINTMENT that evening. Grady opened Ida's door with a flourish, and I had a drink in my hand even before I'd returned his hearty "Hello!" He had me by the elbow in a conciliatory fashion that was comforting in the midst of my flipsided life, and led me to Mrs. Gateway. She reached out to give me a warm hug.

Old friends.

I had assumed correctly that his invitation was for her apartment, although he hadn't exactly told me this. Being brought up proper, I wouldn't have considered being alone in a place so intimate as a man's apartment. I looked at my hand expecting a Heine but the cold drink was a Jolt. *"Twice the caffeine and three times the sugar!"*

"Didn't want you to think we were a couple of lushes." Grady winked. There was a knock on the door. Now, who could that be? I hadn't considered there would be anyone but the three of us that night.

When Ida opened the door Fanny shuffled in, maneuvering her aluminum cart in front of her. After the door closed behind her, she stood upright, lifted the walker into the crook of her arm, and folded it swiftly into a compact mass of metal. Then, she propped it up in a corner, and strode over to Mrs. Gateway where the two hugged tightly. "Can't stand that thing," she said.

The door opened again to admit Bob What-What. Instead of a backward Speedo or pink tutu, he was wearing a pair of khaki Dockers and an Izod pullover. He shook Grady's hand, then turned to me, raised his arms, and said, "What? What?" The small party broke into peels of laughter.

They all looked at me. Grady, Mrs. Gateway, Fanny and Bob then lifted their Jolt cans in a toast, and smiled at one another like they were sharing some kind of perverse secret.

"I don't understand," I said, with no attempt to hide my confusion.

"She's as white as a blanket, poor thing," Ida said.

"I guess you should have given her some clue," Bob said.

"She'll be alright as soon as she knows," Grady said, and came over to touch my shoulder. I jerked away.

"What's going on?" My surprise had turned to anger. What was I, anyway, the butt of some stupid, cruel joke? I didn't like it. Mr. Serling *had* to be around here somewhere.

"She must know by now," Ida said to Grady.

"She has to," Fanny said.

"Look at her. She doesn't have a clue," Bob said.

"She'll figure it out sooner or later, but sooner is better," Grady said.

"May Bell, you take the big chair. Let's have a little talk," Ida said. "I'll get the cookies."

I had that shaky feeling in my legs again, and my stomach was doing the Lambada, so I took a big drink of my Jolt and swallowed a lot of air. The bubbles made my nose zing, and my eyes water. "Thank you," I said after covering a burp with my hand. I felt more naked than I had in my bathing suit. What would my husband have done? He always knew what to do in awkward situations. I could always count on him to say the perfect thing, or to make the perfect exit, while keeping his bridges intact, but he wasn't there. I, on the other hand, *never* knew just what to do, so I simply took my chair and waited. I crossed my legs and smoothed my skirt. If nothing else, I would be a lady.

Grady spoke first. It was clear he was in charge, judging by the quiet, expectant behavior of the others. "We were hoping it had stopped. You're the newest in the complex, but there were several others who moved in over the last few weeks, and we don't think she got to them."

"Probably no reason to," Fanny said.

"There's always a reason; she just hasn't been digging," Bob said.

I found my voice. "Are you still talking about Mrs. Berkowitz?" I leaned forward, placed the can of Jolt on a small round table beside me (complete with real doily) and pressed my palms down on knees to steady their bouncing.

"Of course we're talking about Mrs. Berkowitz." Mrs. Gateway entered and held a steaming plate of cookies. She offered them around. I shook my head because there weren't any handy bushes. Besides, I couldn't have swallowed one if I tried.

Grady rubbed his dark eyebrows with a thumb and forefinger. Everything could have been made all better if he would just take that thumb, hold it up and say, "Just kidding! All a joke!" But when he brought his hand down, I saw that it was trembling.

"You might as well get comfortable, May, because I have a story to tell. It's quite interesting really, because this is one story where we are all the main characters. Are you ready?"

I nodded and leaned forward a bit more. I had to uncross my legs to keep from spilling out onto the floor.

"And whether or not you know it, you're right in the middle of it all. You stepped right in when you signed your lease agreement. No one could have warned you off without giving themselves away. I'm sorry, but we were really hoping it had all stopped. Most of the newbies around here we couldn't care a whit about, but we like you, so we decided you should know the whole story."

"I'm waiting," I said, and it came out sounding a bit snippy; *let's get on with it already*.

Grady smoothed his pant legs with large hands and looked at the others in the room. Ida had taken a place by him on the couch, Bob was straddling a chair, his arms resting on its back, and Fanny was poised on the edge of an ottoman. They had the look of a family gathered around a dying relative.

"Go ahead, man," Fanny said. Her large, round eyes urged the hesitant Grady. "Remember when Mrs. Gateway here said I had left a trail of women and children?"

He put his arm around Mrs. G. and she gently lifted it away. "I was just kidding." Mrs. G. blushed as if she'd been caught with her skirt caught in her girdle, or Depends, or whatever.

"I had a wife, and I have three children. Only married once. I was a banker, that much was true. Retired with the gold watch and everything."

"A good banker, and a good father and husband." Mrs. G. seemed close to tears; her voice was soft. "He couldn't have been anything else."

Grady patted her knee. "I was a good father. And a pretty good husband, but when I was young I did something stupid. I wasn't making much, and we were having kids pretty fast. My wife depended on me for everything, so I was under a lot of pressure. One night I was closing up at the bank and a couple of my friends came by to invite me to a card game. Well, I made some excuse to my wife and stayed pretty much all night at one of the local bars, in the back room playing cards, smoking stogies and talkin' smack."

"Talkin' smack?" That was a new expression.

"You know, just kidding around, having a pretty good time; anyway, the conversation started moving toward money. How to make it, lots of it, and how simple it was to get into this business deal they were hinting at."

"Let me guess," I said. "Not exactly legit."

"Oh, it was legit, all right, at least according to them. I'm not what you'd call naïve, but money pressures can make you do things. It can cloud your judgment."

"What kind of business were they in, Grady?" I pressed, not sure I wanted to hear, but, knowing it was impossible to stop him at this point, I did my best to sound compassionate.

"Imports and sales. These guys had contacts all over. People who made silly little products like key chains, rabbits' feet, sunglasses, watches—you know, trinkets and stuff. They'd buy boxes of the junk and sell them off at hugely inflated prices. It sounded harmless, and by the wads of money they kept throwing around the poker table, I was seduced into wanting a little piece of the action for myself. What did I have to lose?"

"They were looking for investors. Weren't they?" I asked gently.

"Yes. 'Just take out a signature loan, Grady, you'll triple what you borrow and have it all back in the bank in a month,' they told me."

"And you did."

"Naturally. I couldn't afford it, but it seemed like a low-risk deal, and I really needed the money. So I borrowed five thousand dollars. A lot of money in those days. Just signed for it. I put my house up for collateral, but I didn't tell my wife. It was going to be a surprise."

"They stiffed you, didn't they?" I felt a headache coming on.

"No, no, they took my money all right, and in about a week a van drove up to my house and unloaded a crate of boxes. My wife was at the grocery store, and I nearly panicked. She wasn't supposed to know about any of this, so I made a few quick calls and had the stuff taken to a storage unit."

"More money for that."

"Yeah, I was cleaning out my kids' piggy banks. When I started cracking open the boxes, they were all filled with the same stuff. Sunglasses. Hundreds and hundreds of pairs of plain, black, ugly sunglasses. I didn't know who in the world would ever pay for the grotesque things, but I was stuck with them, and had to recoup the money."

"Or goodbye house," Bob said.

"Goodbye Wifey," Fanny said.

"Goodbye kids, job, self-respect," Ida said, sniffing.

"All night I tried to figure out how I was going to sell those hideous glasses.

"Then I had a brainstorm. A brilliant idea! I'd played golf at a nearby country club a few times. I was a guest, since the membership fees were way more than I could afford, but I'd seen a huge pool there, re-membered the tanning golf-wives shielding their eyes and I made some more calls.

"Before you know it, I've got a little table set up at the side of the pool selling sunglasses like nobody's business. They were cheap, disposable, and everyone was snatching them up. Two or three pairs apiece, glasses for the kiddos, the husbands, the wives, the pros; everyone wandered around the place with those repulsive sunglasses on. It was a scorching day, the sun was blazing, and nobody bothered to take their sunglasses off all day. You know, most of the people didn't even swim, they just baked and tanned and posed.

"Good for you," I said.

"Yeah. I almost got away with it. I was down to one box of glasses when I heard some women screaming at the other end of the pool. At first I thought a kid had drowned, the noise was so horrific."

"What was it?" I couldn't even imagine what had gone wrong.

"It was time for everyone to pack up, and people started taking off their glasses. That was when they noticed the cheap, black plastic had melted right onto their skin. The ones who could get the glasses off had huge rings around their eyes and on the bridge of their noses, along the sides of their heads, over their ears. Others were trying to pry off the plastic without much luck. The place was in pandemonium. Kids were sobbing, wives were shouting at their husbands, employees were cursing, and there I was, standing off to the side looking for an avenue of escape. They were mad. Really mad."

"What happened?"

"It was like a mob. They wanted blood, someone to string from the nearest tree. That someone was me. I just left the money and the rest of the glasses and made a break for it. I ran and ran, with the lynch mob screaming for revenge, hot on my heels. We raced the entire golf course at least three times. Most of them had putters or woods in their hands. When I looked behind me, it was a scene I'll never forget. Dozens of people with black rings and red faces shaking their fists. It was like raccoons chasing the hound."

"What about the money?" I asked.

"I lost it all. Nearly lost my house too, but my boss gave me a break and let me work it off. I was so ashamed and embarrassed I never told my wife. She would have been so disappointed."

"But it was just a failed business venture Grady, nothing to be embarrassed about. It happens all the time." To tell you the truth, it was quite comical, but I didn't want to sound unsympathetic.

"That wasn't all." Grady slumped.

"The glasses were stolen. All the goods were stolen. I'd played right into the hands of the biggest con game of the year. The men, my 'friends,' got caught in a sting operation, and it's just luck that they didn't rat me out. And another thing. The money from the bank? Stolen too. I didn't have any collateral; it was all a big lie. The house was my wife's, a gift from her parents. It was a bad thing I'd done."

"But that's over, and I'm sure there's a statute of limitations on the other stuff."

"It's all about personal pride, May. I never want my kids to know I was ever involved in anything so shady. I'd lied, I'd stolen, and I'd taken advantage of others. I just didn't want them to find out."

Grady looked around for strength before going on. "Right after I moved in here, I got an envelope in the mail. In it was a news clipping of the country club group, black rings and all, looking for the man who had put them through all kinds of trauma. After that, I got another news clipping of the con men as they were hauled off to jail. About a week later, I got a letter outlining my involvement, and a request for payment."

"Payment?" I tried to sound confused, but I knew.

"With a bank account number, allotment instructions," Grady said. "Just a little each month. What could it hurt? I have enough to live on, not a lot, but if I save face, it's worth it."

"Payment to whom?" Say it, Grady, say it!

"Shady Grady." Fanny smirked. Ida glared.

"Mrs. Berkowitz. Her son found out, somehow. If he could come up with that, I was sure he could find other things I'm not too proud of. Best to just give her the money and shut her up." Grady looked exhausted.

"Am I to understand Mrs. Berkowitz is extorting money from you for a mistake you made years ago?" All of the heads nodded in unison. "Why should you care? It's done! It's over! You can't go to jail now, all the money was replaced, your wife is gone, so why didn't you just tell her to jump in a lake?"

"My wife never found out, God rest her soul, but my kids don't know," Grady replied.

"It would break their hearts," Mrs. G. said.

"I would do *anything* to keep them from finding out," he continued. "They respect me and I don't want them finding out their father was a thief and a con and that I nearly lost the house because I did something stupid when they were just kids. Besides, if the cops ever found out I was involved in the scam, well, I don't know if I can still be charged in something like this."

"So she's taking hush money?" Don't know where I learned that phrase, but it seemed appropriate.

"From all of us." Fanny said. Her face was screwed up into a mixture of disgust and worry.

"All of you?" I shouldn't have sounded surprised; I'd seen the list of names. The pregnancies, the abortions, the secrets. Then I remembered my name, followed by *second marriage illegal*.

As if reading my thoughts, Grady asked, "May, is there any reason you need to worry?"

It was time to spill all. I knew they were telling the truth about my neighbor, and I had to trust them. "I'm married." I said, and waited for them all to appear shocked. They didn't. "I was married before, but my husband disappeared in combat. I thought he was dead." I poured out everything Mrs. Berkowitz already knew. I found myself talking in a rush, pouring out the details of my separation from my current husband, and the possibility that my marriage was all a sham.

"Then if anyone finds out, you won't get anything in the divorce." Fanny said frowning.

"And your husband is quite wealthy, I take it?" Mrs. G. added.

"He's a surgeon."

"Makes loads," Bob said.

"A bundle," Fanny said.

"Not to mention she's a bigot!" Ida said. "That's only legal in Utah, you know."

"Just the thing to keep you from saying a word when she starts demanding money," Fanny said.

"Lady, you've got problems," Grady said, bringing down the gavel.

"But how does she do it? Doesn't anyone say anything? She could be put in jail for such things." I wondered how I would explain any of this to my daughter, and understood why people were reluctant to report the old witch.

"Word has it that her son, the guy who visits now and then, is a retired private investigator. He's got his fingers in a lot of pies," Grady said.

"Mud pies," Ida huffed.

"Forget scruples. Those guys can find out anything about anyone, anywhere." Grady agreed.

"How long has this been going on?" I asked, trying to absorb the implications of it all.

"She moved in here about three years ago. I got a

peek at her file one day, just curious, and found out she never lives anywhere for long. She's moved around a lot, and my suspicion is, that she's dipped into a lot of purses along the way." Bob What-What was talking. "Nobody pays much attention to me, so I can get in and out of places pretty easily." This made everyone laugh. "Remember, I'm crazy. It's a bonus when you need it."

I shook my head; the fuzzy feeling was returning. "So when she leaves, it all stops?"

"We don't know." Grady stood up and stretched. There were twin stains under his armpits. "And we don't know how many people she's taking money from, but one thing's for sure, nobody's talking. We all have families, and we all have a history. Nobody wants to air their dirty laundry, especially at this stage in life."

"Maybe if we were younger, we'd take her on," Mrs. Gateway said, her eyes on Grady. "But we just want to finish our lives in peace. Mostly, we don't want anyone to get hurt."

"This is absurd!" I grabbed my Jolt and took a swig. I waved it around. "Somebody has to stop her."

"Don't forget that son of hers. We're fairly certain she's just a go-between. He's the real head of this operation. The money filters through her, and then somewhere, probably into a Swiss bank account, or lost in the Caymans. Who knows? There's a lot more to this operation than we're aware of, and I don't imagine that guy is careless enough to leave things to chance. He's probably covered his tail pretty good." Grady sat down again. He had obviously thought this out.

"Not quite," I said. All eyes turned to me. "He didn't consider one thing." Eyebrows went up.

"What's that honey?" Ida asked.

I looked around to be sure they were all listening, and then said, "Me."

TEN

MY COMMENT LANDED like a brick, and then I was attacked. *What do you mean? What are you saying? Do you know something new?* I enjoyed the attention for a while, knowing I was just about to add a new dimension to the machinations of our dear Mrs. Berkowitz. It felt good to know I had an ace up my sleeve. "Where did you put my purse?" I asked Ida.

Mrs. Gateway looked flustered. "I put it in the closet. Just a minute, I'll get it."

I nearly ripped the purse from her hands when she held it out. I felt for the diskette, couldn't find it for a brief frightening moment, rummaged fretfully, and then had my fingers around it. I pulled the diskette out and held it aloft. "I'm talking about this. Do you have a computer?" I waved it at Ida, who took a step back and shook her head.

"Do you?" I looked at Grady.

"I have an old one, don't use it much."

"Does it have a printer?" My words were coming out fast. This was getting good.

"Dot matrix, it's slow but it works."

"Let's go." I headed for the door with the party in

tow. We raced down the steps and crowded into Thumbs' apartment. His computer took forever to boot up, but eventually we had everything working. The printer shuffled along, spitting out sheet after sheet of printed paper.

Hands grabbed up the papers and there were muttered expletives, emissions of surprise, exclamations all around me, murmuring, mumbling, so much stir I have to admit I felt a satisfied tingle, being the source of all of this agitation.

"Where did you get this?" Grady asked. He had one sheet clenched in his fist, the enormity of Mrs. Berkowitz's operation hitting hard. "Has she somehow gotten you involved?"

"Say it isn't so, May." Ida furrowed her brow and gave me a look similar to one my second grade teacher gave when she found me cheating on a spelling test.

"What? No!" I sputtered. "Grady, remember when I told you I was getting a new computer and I was going to ask Mrs. Berkowitz to help me set it up?"

"And I told you to stay away."

"Well, you weren't exactly forthcoming with the reasons. Everyone was acting so crazy, and I wanted to find out what all the deal was for myself."

"I still don't see how you got this stuff," Mrs. Gateway said. Her face was drawn and pale.

"I didn't steal it, if that's what you're thinking. I accidentally took it home with some other diskettes I had been working with."

"Oh! Oh no, May Bell, she might know you have it! This could complicate everything. What do you think she'll do when she finds out?" Ida was clinging to Grady's arm, and I looked around for a chair. I didn't want her sitting on the floor.

"I don't think she'll know right away. She said she had transferred all of her stuff onto CDs."

"Pretty careless of her to keep this lying around." Grady put a hand over Mrs. Gateway's knuckles and rubbed.

"She probably had it out, getting ready to destroy the evidence," Fanny said.

"No. It was a plant. She wanted May to find it. Maybe she put it in May's purse." Bob had his arms resting on top of his belly.

"That doesn't make any sense. What good would that do? She hasn't sent me any of those letters and I surely haven't given her any money." It all sounded so ridiculous.

"Fate," Fanny whispered.

"Karma," Bob said.

"Accident," I said.

"Now the thing is, you've got to get this back into her apartment without her seeing. That's not going to be too easy. Do you have a plan?" Grady pulled a toothpick out of his pocket and began to chew on it while propping up Mrs. G.

I sighed heavily. "I'll get it back. But that's not the issue here. We've got to put a stop to all of this baloney.

I'm going to make a copy of this and take it to the police tomorrow."

"NO!" All four screamed out in chorus.

"You can't do that! We'll all be exposed, and then our kids will know, our grandkids; some of the things on here have no statute of limitations. Some of these people could go to jail." Mrs. Gateway groaned and sagged. I got a chair under her just in time.

"So we just let her keep on doing what she's doing?" I asked.

"I don't see any other way. I'd rather give her part of my Social Security check every month to keep all this under wraps, thank you very much." Fanny took off her glasses and blew on them. She rubbed them with a corner of her blouse. "I can play the cripple until she moves on."

"And what is that all about?" I turned to her. "You look like you can run a marathon right now. Why the walker?"

"I golf for money. Under an assumed name of course. I've been on the circuit and you should see me putt." Fanny waved her arms, doing a mock swing. I looked on with my flabbers gasted. "I don't want her digging into my life any more than she does. This just throws her off a bit."

"When in the world do you ever have time?" I asked. It was just all too much to swallow.

Fanny blinked at me with those enormous eyes. "Bob here's not the only one who gets around. And while he's causing the distractions and the other babes are doing tea, I'm teeing up!" I could tell Fanny was getting hot under her lace collar. Just let it be, May Bell.

"You want me to go with you when you slip that floppy back into the old hag's hooch?" Grady asked. He was rubbing his knuckles, and it appeared he was gearing up for an old-fashioned roughing up.

"No!" I grabbed the diskette and threw it back into my purse. "No, no, I can manage."

"I'll provide the distraction." Bob What-What looked at the others for confirmation. They all bobbed their gray heads.

"You'll know what to do!" Mrs. Gateway clapped her hands together again, the trained seal flap. Color was seeping back into her cheeks.

"No," I said firmly. "Keep your shirt on Bob. And your pants. Please. I'll make up some excuse and she'll let me in. I took her some snacks earlier, and that's just the excuse I need to go calling. She might need some milk or something."

"Gooood May. Just run right over there. 'Here's your milk, and by the way, here's the little diskette I stole, so's I could find out about all your evil doings.'" Grady winked and put a thumb up, but it was a sarcastic thumb this time. I wanted to twist it off.

"Knock it off, Grady. You're not the only one who knows what to do with a floppy." Mrs. Gateway lifted an eyebrow at him. I could imagine her giving that look to a wayward student. It worked.

"Not to mention a hard drive!" Grady was grinning back at Mrs. Gateway, and she swatted at him.

"Let's just end this right now before you start talking about downloading. I couldn't bear it," I said. Ida blushed then, because we were all rolling our eyes.

The mood was light again, and we knew it was time to break up the party. On the way out of the apartment, everyone was looking at me as if it was for the last time. They were patting me on the back, giving me the big send off. I set off down the sidewalk alone, the thing in my purse feeling like a loaded gun. I could do this. When I was clear of the cheering section, my footsteps slowed. I was moving along the lighted path by sheer momentum, and I had never felt so alone. I couldn't remember the last time I'd eaten anything, and the Jolt went straight to the end of my nerve fibers, causing me to tremble all over. First a bite of Very Berry and I'd be fine. But then I remembered I'd flushed all of my junk food, nearly causing a panic. My husband wasn't around to lean on anymore, my rum raisin crutch was gone, and it was just me. All me.

"It's all me," I whispered to the flowered bushes. "Yeah. Nobody else to direct my paths, choose how I should walk, or talk, or act in public; nobody around to correct me when I use the wrong fork or wear a slip too long for my dress, or to tell me to stand up straight. Just me. And to prove it, I took an extra leisurely lap around the complex just to show who was boss. And then I took another.

ELEVEN

As I STOOD IN FRONT OF Mrs. Berkowitz's door, I had one of those out-of-body experiences I'd once read about in *Cosmopolitan,* or *Redbook,* or maybe it was *Good Housekeeping.* The article said that in the face of extreme danger, your senses become so inhumanly acute that you have the ability to do things no mortal could do with any plausible explanation. On the other hand, too much excitement and women have been known to faint. I wasn't feeling so good. Felt a little like I was gonna barf. Breathe, May Bell, breathe.

Even before I rapped on number 3C, there was a tension in the air, something different about the way the world felt, which is saying a lot, since the litany of changes I'd gone through lately had run the gamut. I knew she could hear me knocking, because Paco was silent for a change, and there wasn't a ukulele to be heard. All quiet on the wrinkled front. I knocked again, just in case she truly hadn't heard me, because by now the old smarmy eyes should have been giving me the once-over. She knew I'd be back. She was just letting me suffer out there on the landing. Uh oh. She'd been tipped off. That was it! Why else would she be taking so long? She was in there, shredding documents or copying files. Who knew what she did behind those doors? Well, I wasn't about to let her. I was going in. Look out Mrs. Berkowitz, the jig is up! I grabbed the door handle, and in the face of everything insane, I gave a giant shove.

The door wasn't locked. It wasn't even latched. I fell forward into the living room and threw my arms out to catch my fall, but my own weight sent me barreling to the floor. My solar plexus hit something soft and hard at the same time. When I opened my eyes I was staring into the face of Mrs. Berkowitz, her scrabbly, gnarled fist curled under my abdomen. I tried to cry out, but with no air, I opened and closed my mouth like the fish I'd hooked last summer at Tahoe. I pushed away, and got to a crawl position, struggling to make sense of what I saw.

There she was, the old lady of the underworld, legs splayed out in a V, her plaid skirt up to her thighs, exposing her bitty, round knees. Her eyes were wide open, and so was her mouth. Her arms were out in a relaxed "I give" fashion, and it didn't take a doctor, or even a doctor's wife, to spot the obvious. The German clock announced the hour then, and I couldn't help but say aloud, "Ding-dong—the 'Witz is dead."

What to do? What to do? Get to the phone. Call the police.

I donkey-kicked the door closed, had the phone in my hand in a flash, ready to make the 911 call, when

I remembered it wasn't connected to anything. Darn. I'd have to use the one in my apartment. That was okay; I didn't really want to be in the same room with *the body* anyway. It was the right thing to do. Leave, call the authorities, and let them take care of business.

That's what I *should* have done. But I didn't. I stood there, staring at the old lady on the floor, thinking about the other room and what I might find if I just took a few minutes. Calm, May Bell, calm. Every muscle in my body was a-quiver. Did I dare? I could take a peek, it wouldn't hurt anything, I'd just get in there, slip a few disks into my purse, maybe bring up some menus, maybe just do some erasing of my own. I stared at the old woman again, thinking she might be playing a trick. It would be just like her to go for the ultimate surprise. The minute my fingers were on her keyboard, I'd see her form in the blank screen, her mouth in a panting, snarling grimace; she'd grab my collar, and just as I opened my mouth to scream bloody murder, she'd attack. I nudged her thigh with the toe of my shoe.

Knock! Knock! Knock! If I'd had false teeth, I'd have swallowed them. The knocking at the door sounded like three sonic booms. I jumped free of my skin, then pulled it back together and whirled around to face the front door. It was creeping open, slowly pushing inward.

"What? What?"

"Bob!" I squeaked, and hurdled Mrs. Berkowitz.

Bob was looking over my shoulder. Gone were the khaki Dockers and sensible shirt; he had changed into a black teddy. I hauled him in. "Don't step on her," I said, and threw the door closed one more time.

"What is this? You killed her?" Bob smiled, and a look of admiration crossed his face. He hunkered down, and got close to Mrs. Berkowitz's face.

"Of course I killed her. I just didn't see any other way... No! I didn't kill her; she was like this when I got here. Bob, what are you wearing?"

"Thought you might need a little distraction."

"I told you I didn't. Can't you put something else on? I can't think."

"Have you called anyone?"

"I was going to call 911, but her phone doesn't work."

"Good," Bob said. He got to one knee and put two fat fingers on her eyelids. "There. That's better; sort of creepy isn't she?" Mrs. Berkowitz's leaky eyes were closed forever. I gagged a little.

"What's that brown stuff around her mouth?" Bob asked. He was still staring at the old woman.

"Probably blood. I don't know." I stared at the aquarium, watching the little scuba diver. I didn't feel like looking at Mrs. Berkowitz anymore.

"I don't think so." I pulled my eyes back to Bob, and took a step closer. He put a finger to the corner of Mrs. Berkowitz's mouth and dabbed. Then he put his finger to his tongue. I gagged hard that time.

"It's sweet!" Bob looked up at me. "Chocolate!"

"Chocolate?" I looked around wildly. "The brownies!"

"Hmm?" Bob reached down to swab a little more.

"Stop!" I cried. "Oh my God, oh my God, I brought her brownies. They were right here!" I searched the living room, and then rushed to the kitchen. On the counter was the empty plate. On the plate was a dusting of dried crumbs, the only evidence there had been brownies at all. I walked the plate back to the living room.

"She ate them all?" Bob asked.

"If she was diabetic, she probably OD'd. I guess I have killed her," I said. I pressed my fist to my mouth. How many Hail Marys would this cost me?

"Don't be ridiculous," Bob said, getting to his feet. "You didn't hold a gun to her head." He clucked his tongue and took another look at Mrs. Berkowitz. "Death for dessert."

All the tension boiled over. I started laughing. The vision of Bob in his black teddy, together with the whole sordid mess of my life, just seemed so crazy that my legs were turning to noodles and I sank to the floor, laughing so hard I couldn't breathe. I may have spotted. *Ding-dong, the 'Witz is dead.* The clock chimed the quarter hour.

When I could finally get my voice back, I asked Bob what we should do. Now that I wasn't alone, the idea of getting to her files wasn't quite so daunting. I was hoping he knew something about computers so we could do what we had to do, and get the heck out of hell.

"Let me think a minute." Bob paced around *the body,* his hand stroking his chin. "You know what we've got here? We've got a chance to take our lives back!"

"That's what I was thinking. Let's get into her computers and just delete all that stuff."

"That's no good. If her son has been feeding all of this stuff to her, he's got to have copies. He'll just find another way to keep this operation going."

"We don't know that," I was suddenly whispering. The mariachi music was starting up downstairs. "We've got to try."

"Okay. I suppose you're right. But I want to get the rest of the gang in on this. Go call Grady and tell him to hurry over with Fanny and Ida. We can figure out what to do together."

I couldn't wait to get out of there. I punched in Grady's number. "Call the gang and get everyone over to Mrs. Berkowitz's apartment immediately! This is an emergency!" I hung up the phone before any questions. I hoped my phone wasn't tapped, and thought it would have been better if I'd been more cryptic. Too late for that now. Back across the landing, I opened the door more carefully, not wanting to trip over little dead feet, but Mrs. Berkowitz was gone.

I heard Bob grunting in the hallway, and found myself saying, "What? What?" Bob had the old woman under the arms, dragging her backwards. Her heels left grooves in the brown carpet, and her hair had fallen off. I picked up the wig, the gray fluffy one, and followed Bob into the computer room.

"No bed?" Bob was huffing.

"No bed."

Bob let go, and Mrs. Berkowitz hit the floor hard.

"You can't just leave her here!" I pointed with the wig.

"Where then?"

"Put her in the closet." I pushed the louvered doors apart. This was one nutty woman. She had at least a dozen wigs hanging on hooks along the walls, shoes from every generation were placed side by side, and outfits that looked more like costumes hung in clear plastic bags.

"Should I put her in one of those bags?" Bob asked.

"What? No! Just get her out of the way. She's looking at me again." One of Mrs. Berkowitz's eyes had crept open, and she was staring. I could almost hear her say, *Do you have an answer for me yet?* Here's your answer, you old bat. I grabbed her ankles and started pulling. "Get her arms, Bob!"

We had her folded into the closet when the knock came. I checked the peephole. All clear. "Get in here." I grabbed Grady and pulled him in. "Where's everyone else?"

"They're on their way. Fanny's got her walker so she's taking her time."

"Oh for Pete's sake." I looked out at the walkway and could see a shadow bumping along. A bigger shadow behind her must be Mrs. Gateway.

"What's this all about? Where's…" Grady wagged his eyebrows.

"Let's wait for everybody. Hold your horses," I said, wishing the women would hurry. I could hear Paco starting up. The last thing I wanted was to see the shiny glimmer of Mr. Mariachi's tooth in the twilight. Well, if that happened, we'd just put Bob to work. I hadn't seen Mr. Greenjeans lately, and that was another thing to worry about. He always had a way of lurking around at the most inopportune times. Hurry up, Fanny!

I waved a frantic "come hither" when the women were at the bottom of the stairs. Fanny glanced around and threw her walker over her shoulder. She took the stairs in twos. Mrs. Gateway was at her heels.

"What's going on?" Fanny asked. She was breathless and excited. Her eyes were wider than usual, if that were at all possible.

"Is everything alright?" Mrs. Gateway looked around, searching for Mrs. Berkowitz.

"Don't worry. She's not here," I said. "At least, not exactly." I felt the bubble rise again and didn't want to lose control. Laughing with a corpse in the room was, undeniably, not proper.

Bob came out of the bedroom/computer center. His teddy was riding high on his hairy, thunder thighs. One of the thin straps had fallen. *Oh crap. Here I go.* I doubled over, and everyone stared as if I'd lost my mind. Well, maybe I had. I dabbed my eyes and got control a little faster than before.

"What is going on?" Fanny was losing her patience fast. I pointed at Bob, a signal that he should explain. I was afraid to say anything; the bubble was still just below the surface.

"Just come here," Bob said, and turned around. The back teddy vision didn't help matters. I went boneless again.

I waited in the living room, taking deep breaths, clearing my throat, waiting, waiting, and then I heard the gasps, the *"Oh my Lord,"* the *"Is she dead?"* And the confirming grunts of Bob before he shut the closet doors again. The group came back into the living room, moving like they'd all had lobotomies. They sat down on the furniture, hands folded in laps—a moment of silence.

"Who found her?" Grady asked.

I raised a hand.

"In the closet?" Fanny asked. Her forehead was wrinkled up, line upon line.

I pointed to the floor.

"Well, how did she get in there?" Mrs. Gateway asked.

Bob raised his hand. "But it was her idea. She helped."

"What did you do that for?" Fanny asked.

"To tell you the truth, I don't know." I shrugged.

"It doesn't matter," Bob said. "What we have here is a chance to get at her stuff. I say we clean 'er out, and then put her body back where it was. Then we call 911."

"Why in tarnation did you call us over here? This all sounds illegal, if you ask me. I mean fiddling with a dead body, going through her stuff, this is wrong!" Mrs. Gateway clutched the collar of her pink cotton sweater.

"And what she did was *legal?* Really. We're all in this together. We can all help. The more the better— only, what we do here tonight stays here. Kapeesh?" Bob looked at us all in turn.

"Kapeesh," I said. "What now?"

"Grady, you know more about computer stuff than any of us," Bob said. "We need you at the keyboard. May Bell, you're the cleanup crew. Get rid of the brownie plate."

"That's how she died," I explained to the puzzled looks. "We think she's diabetic. Death by brownie." Stop it May, steady, steady. My eyes were tearing up and I covered them with a hand, pretending to be saddened. My throat was making a mmm sound and a bray was on the rise.

"May? You gave her your brownies?" Ida was one shade whiter than the corpse in the closet. It was strange how upset she was, as if I had done it on purpose, meaning to "off" the bat. I thought we'd gotten that cleared up. Apparently I hadn't convinced Ida; she kept changing colors on me.

"If they do an autopsy they'll know. They always find out," Fanny said in a rush. "I've watched 'Perry Mason' enough. I know these things."

"Doesn't matter. We just can't have May Bell's plate linked. For all they'll know she got the brownies on free bread day," Bob said.

"But they'll check and find out there weren't any brownies at free bread day. They always check those things." Fanny was on a roll.

Ida wandered over to the spineless books and kept rubbing the leather. I think she was in her own little world at that point. Maybe we were witnessing a fugue state first hand.

"So what? She wasn't murdered, they only check those things if they assume foul play." Bob was getting impatient. The clock dinged the hour, a reminder that time was slipping away. "Fanny, you're lookout. If anyone comes up this way, you just say Mrs. Berkowitz is indisposed. That'll take care of any visitors."

"She never has visitors," I assured Fanny. "So you won't need to worry."

"There's that son of hers, comes around at strange times," Grady said.

"We'll handle that if we have to," Bob said. "Just keep your eyes peeled, Fanny. Stand out on the balcony. Can you whistle?"

Fanny shook her head. "Not since I got new teeth."

"Just do something if you see anyone coming up the stairs."

"What should I do?" Mrs. Gateway was back, more or less. She'd found the couch and was shrinking into it.

"Make us some coffee," Bob said, and motioned for Grady to follow him into the computer center.

"But they'll know she didn't make the coffee!

They'll be able to trace spittle from the cups! They always check those things!" Fanny said.

Bob looked impatient and held out his hands. "That's why you have your story ready. When the paramedics come, we'll tell them we made coffee while we waited. Just get to your post." Fanny looked insulted and pushed open the balcony door.

Ida walked like a zombie to the kitchen. "She could be right about some of this stuff," I said cautiously. "We'll need to come up with a story. And we shouldn't all be here when the cops come, or whoever comes to a thing like this. It would be strange."

"Later. We'll get a story together later. Right now turn off all the lights in the living room. We don't want to attract attention," Bob said.

I flipped off the lights and heard Fanny peep. Mrs. Gateway absently opened and closed cabinet doors. Soon I could hear the soft gurgle of the coffee maker. And I thought Mrs. B. only did tea.

We were all on the second pot of coffee two hours later when Grady leaned back in the chair, and ran his hands through his hair for the hundredth time. His eyes were red-rimmed, his underarms soaked.

"This is going to take longer than I thought," he said. It sounded like a request for forgiveness. "The files are all passworded and I can't find a back door." We'd all been hovering, pacing, taking an occasional peek into the closet to see if Mrs. Berkowitz hadn't made a miraculous recovery.

"What do we do now?" Fanny had long ago abandoned her post, assuring us that nothing was moving out there except the mosquitoes. Grady looked exhausted. "I say we steal her CPU and all of her disks, wait 'til first light, then find someone who can break the code. We replace everything with exact replicas and let the microchips fall where they may."

Fanny snorted. "Won't that be a bit suspicious if her son decides to do some looking and finds there's nothing on her computer?"

"Not to mention his dead mother stuffed in the closet." Bob snickered.

Grady was thinking. "Yeah, but it won't be like that. I'll get the files off of her CPU and download everything back on the new stuff—except anything that can be incriminating. What's he going to do? Tell the police someone took the secret extortion files?"

"We still have the problem of…" I jerked my head toward the hall.

"Has anyone seen Bob lately?" Mrs. Gateway had been quietly sitting with her coffee cup until then. We all looked at one another and shrugged. A toilet flushed nearby.

"Had to take a leak, I guess," Grady said, and started pulling cables.

"He's been in there an awful long time." Ida looked genuinely worried.

"Had to take more than a leak?" Grady rolled his eyes up and to the right.

"Oh, they can trace that kind of stuff! He should have gone to your apartment, May Bell, why couldn't he hold it?" Fanny was revving up.

"I don't think we have to worry about that," I assured her, but Bob still hadn't come out of the bathroom and I caught a bit of the worry worm with Mrs. G., who was leaning an ear toward the door.

"Bob, you okay in there?" Grady called out.

"Bob?" Mrs. G. echoed.

Bob came out, his face ashen, his eyes bloodshot. He had spittle on his mouth and he didn't look good.

"Bob? Is everything okay?" I hurried over to him. "Confounded stomach. Something I ate I think, I'm feeling a bit queasy."

I felt a cold finger of fear tap me on the shoulder.

"It's all the excitement, I'm sure. It's not every day that you fold a dead woman into her wardrobe." Mrs. G. was consoling. At least *she* was looking closer to normal. I shot a look at the brownie plate, still resting on the kitchen counter. The sensation was growing, now thumping me in the chest.

"Maybe that's it," Bob said. He was positively green.

"Bob." I caught his attention. "Did you eat any of the brownie crumbs off of the plate?"

Mrs. G. slapped a hand over her mouth and said, "Oh!"

"What? What?" Bob said, but with greatly diminished gusto.

I ran over to the plate and lifted it. Much less cluttered than I had remembered. "Here, this, did you eat anything off of this plate?"

"Just a couple of crumbs, that's all." Bob looked thunderstruck. "Oh, God," he said. His eyes were wide with fear.

"Go throw up Bob; put your finger down your throat, do whatever you have to do, just make yourself throw up. I think Mrs. Berkowitz died from the brownies alright, but it wasn't the sugar that killed her."

I didn't need to encourage him further; Bob was down the hall, retching into the toilet before I could finish my sentence.

Grady winced. "Can't you at least close the door?" He had the CPU under his arm and was wrapping up the cords with the help of Mrs. G. Fanny did us the favor of pulling the bathroom door shut.

"There was something in those brownies, wasn't there?" Fanny's glasses were fogging, and she pulled them off to give a wipe before resetting them on her nose. "They'll do tests on those, and they'll think it was us, for sure." She grabbed a dishtowel and started wiping down the apartment. "Fingerprints," she said. "They'll do a full fiber test, vacuum the carpet and furniture. I'd better bring over my Shop-Vac just in case." She was working up a frenzy and I didn't stop her. Was it true? Could we be implicated in something dastardly?

Bob came out of the bathroom, wiping his face with a tissue. He looked like he was over the worst of it, but who knew?

"Take that with you!" Fanny shouted, pointing to the tissue. "Then, when you get to your apartment, boil it, then flush it."

"For heaven's sake Fanny, it's just a Kleenex," Bob said. He hitched up the spaghetti straps of his teddy. The silk front was stained and wet. I wasn't laughing anymore.

"They can do a full chem. analysis, find out what was in those brownies, and they'll know you just chucked up some yourself."

Bob looked grim. "I think I'm going on a diet," he said.

Grady set the computer parts by the door and turned to all of us, now huddled together in the living room. "Look. We're all tired, it's late, and we're still not done. I'm bushed and want to go to bed, so listen up. First, we get Mrs. Berkowitz out of the closet."

That prompted a group groan.

"She's got to sleep somewhere. Find her bed, and put her on it. She's an old woman, and if my guess is right, they'll just think she's died in her sleep. It's cool enough in here to keep her from smelling up the place until we finish what we have to do."

More groans.

"I have to find someone who's better at this computer stuff. I couldn't break through the passwords. I'll try again tomorrow, then we'll get her stuff back."

I raised my hand. "When I bought my computer, I met someone who might be able to help us."

"Can he be trusted?" Fanny asked.

"I think I can make up something good. He thinks I'm an idiot. That should count for something."

"Dear," Mrs. Gateway said, patting my back gently, "you're not an idiot. Don't let him treat you like one."

Grady mulled over my suggestion. We were clearly out of options, but he didn't want to fumble over a half-baked plan. He didn't think long before coming up with a solution. "So it doesn't sound suspicious, you take the CPU into the store, tell him you got it cheap but you want to free-up some of the hard drive. You could even say you got it from a relative who died suddenly, and so you don't have the password. If he's as good as you think he is, he'll be able to find a back door."

"Just make sure he doesn't erase anything. Tell him to copy it to a disk or to a CD." Bob was looking better. The finger down the throat must have worked.

"What should we do about that?" I pointed to the brownie plate. "If she died of natural causes that's one thing, but if there's something in them, and she was murdered, then we have a whole mystery to solve." Fanny seemed to be enjoying herself.

"Who would want to kill Mrs. Berkowitz?" Mrs. G. asked, sweet Mrs. G.

"Who wouldn't?" We all answered in unison.

"Oh," she said.

"May," Grady said, suddenly looking at me as if he'd caught me shoplifting. "Didn't you say you'd brought her those brownies?"

All eyes swung around to me.

"Oh, you didn't, May, please say you didn't!" Mrs. G. had her hand over her mouth again.

"No! It's not what you think! I brought her the brownies, yes, but they were left for me, on my step. I thought the Mariachis had left them. They're always leaving me stuff. I went on a diet and that's why I gave them to Mrs. Berkowitz!" I was spilling out an explanation, worried that they really could think I'd snuffed the witch, when I was struck with another thought. I said in a whisper. "They were for me."

"Hoo boy." Bob threw his hands in the air and did a one-eighty. I couldn't tell if he was thinking I was the biggest liar in the world, or if he was thinking, like *I* was, that it should have been me sprawled on the floor sporting a chocolate grin.

"Well who would want you dead?" Fanny asked. She had her arms crossed, waiting, I suppose, for some explanation. I didn't have one. Instead, I felt tears welling up, and I just wanted to go home. Not to the place across the hall, but home. My *real* home.

I sniffed loudly. "I'm calling 911."

"Wait. Just wait a minute." Mrs. G. was talking quickly. "We've got some loose ends, that's true. But we're a smart bunch; we can figure all of this out. We're just tired. Everything will look brighter in the morning."

"Brighter for you!" I was sniffing really loudly now. "Nobody wants you dead!"

"It was all a mistake, I'm sure. Just a mistake." Mrs. G. was rubbing my back again. It made me feel a little better. At least they didn't think I was a liar and a murderess. I was brought up proper, and if I were to kill someone, I certainly wouldn't have done it with poisonous brownies. Electrocution maybe, but not brownies.

"We're all a bit punchy. It's understandable," Bob said. "And I'm chafing. Let's get Mrs. Berkowitz out of the closet, clean up, and get out of here. We'll meet tomorrow morning at Mrs. G.'s house. Say eightish?"

"Free bread day, don't forget," Fanny said.

"Alright. After free bread."

TWELVE

WE WRESTLED MRS. BERKOWITZ out of the closet. No easy task, since she'd begun to hit rigor. Fanny and I had her feet while the men took an arm apiece. She was frozen in a sitting position and she was winking at us again.

"This is no good. We've got to straighten her out," Bob said.

"On the count of three, give a tug," Grady said.

On three we pulled her like toffee and she did straighten a bit. Her spine let out a string of soft, little pops. Better than a chiropractor. She hadn't been adjusted like that in years, I'd bet. Since we hadn't found a bed, we made do with the couch. Mrs. G. ran for an afghan and tucked it around the corpse. Soon the old woman was comfortable, even had her feet propped on a pillow after Bob took off her shoes. There was the wig, and I didn't know if she slept with it on or off, so I just hung it over a lampshade. *Bald as an onion!*

"This'll look good." Fanny, all business, opened a book and laid it down on Mrs. Berkowitz's chest. It was one of the books from her shelf, the ones with no titles. Just because I was curious, I tilted the book and glanced. There were words in it, after all. I flipped to the cover page. *I'm Okay, You're Okay.* Should have been called, *I'm Dead, You're Not.*

I placed it back on her chest. "Nice touch, Fanny."

We wiped, and cleaned, and, at last, determined everything was in generally good order. I even straightened the closet. Anything left undone we'd just have to explain away when we got our story straight.

Bob disappeared into his apartment, Grady walked the gals home, and I went straight to my refrigerator. Darn. Some habits are hard to break.

I should have crashed like a wingless 707, but there was just too much going on in my head, not to mention the box fans whirring like a tempest at the end of my bed. The gang had left it up to me to take the brownie plate, and I suppose that meant I was going to need to order some kind of analysis to answer the big question. Why would someone want me dead? What would my husband have done?

"May, May, May. Do you always have to be so melodramatic? There's no need to worry. To prove it, I'll take the plate to my lab and let them have a look-see. There's this new little technician down there with a lot of promise. I'm sure she won't have any qualms about running a few test tubes through the centrifuge. She's handled my tubes plenty of times and I haven't complained about her performance yet!"

Perhaps I was being melodramatic. The brownies may have been full of nothing more than sugar, chocolate, and calories. Bob may have just been suffering from indigestion; Mrs. Berkowitz may have had an insulin upset. They'd just been another hospitable gesture from the Mariachis. Tomorrow I'd return the plate and watch their reactions. Being cautious, I scraped all that was left of the crumbs into a Ziploc, and rinsed the plate.

I had to keep up appearances the next day. It was important to make things look normal—not to draw suspicion. I got dressed early, ate a tasteless apple, put on some lipstick with a shaky hand, gave up on the mascara after three failed attempts and a jab in the eye, which hurt quite a bit, and sat on the edge of my bed watching the clock. When I heard the music downstairs, I decided it was time. I started for the door with the plate in hand, but my feet were dragging. What if it wasn't a gift from Anita? What if it was? What if I had some crazed killers living under my floor, systematically poisoning old folks in the Senior Center? No sense equivocating about it, I reminded myself I was a different May these days, and I wasn't about to let a couple of little brownies do me in. I opened the door and had a spasm. The Mariachis were standing in front of my door; Mr. Mariachi had one fist raised, level with my left cheek.

"May Bell!" Mr. Mariachi said. Blast that little, gold toothed, grinning, brown man. "I was just about to knock. Came to remind you it's free bread day. Don't be late!"

The pair almost got away. I collected myself and shouted at them, giving Mrs. Mariachi a good verbal whiplash.

"Wait!" I held the plate out. "I just wanted to return your plate." Then as an afterthought, "I'm sorry but I dropped the brownies, and had to throw them away. They looked delicious though."

Mrs. Mariachi frowned and shook her head. "That's not my plate." She turned to her husband. "Is that my plate? I don't remember that plate."

"No, not our plate." Mr. Mariachi said. "But we can bring up some Pico de Gallo later, Anita makes the best Pico de Gallo. No scrimping on the cilantro. As soon as we get our bread."

I thanked them and promised to get down to the Senior Center right away. At least, I'd answered that question, but things weren't any less confusing than before. I would need to stop jumping to conclusions. I'd just get the brownie crumbs analyzed and find out there was nothing to worry about. Yes. Nothing at all to worry about.

I couldn't help but envision Mrs. Berkowitz lying on her couch next door, her hair hanging on the lampshade, her feet propped on a pillow, a book on her chest. She was probably stiff as a board by now, her face looking like last night's sunset. I was really glad she didn't have a cat. That would have been really creepy, the cat curled up on its master's neck, purring away, or maybe howling like cats do because they know things, and a cat would have announced to the world my guilt in all of this.

Grady caught my eye as soon as I entered the Free Bread melee. I made nice as I did a sashay over to his side of the room, tipping my head to a woman I recognized, accepting the outstretched hand of a man wearing a hat full of fishing hooks, smiling nicely to a lady overflowing from her wheelchair. *The last thing she needed was more bread,* I thought, and then felt bad for thinking that.

"Where's everyone else?" I stage whispered. There was so much commotion I had to get close to Grady's ear. I saw gray hairs poking out of his lobe.

"Fanny's come and gone already. She gets first dibs because of her *disability*." I smiled at this. So there was more to that clattery old walker than just a mere distraction.

"I'll bet she gets good parking at the supermarket too," I said.

"Well, if you ever need to do any shopping, catch a ride with Fanny. She never has to circle the block."

Just then, I saw Mrs. Gateway near the back of the room. She was stretching her neck, looking over the sea of blue hair and looked relieved when she saw Grady lift a thumb in the air to catch her attention. She caught up with us before the geriatric sea pulled her into its rip tide and, fortunately, at that moment there was a tremendous squabble in front, an argument over some coveted croissants, which afforded us a bit of privacy.

"I couldn't sleep all night," Mrs. Gateway said. She was clearly exhausted, her eyes were puffy with dark bags hanging below them, and her hair was in disarray. I noticed her cotton housedress was inside out, but if you didn't look closely you wouldn't have been able to tell. I just hoped she'd gotten her Depends on right. I placed my hand over the tag on her back and wondered how in the world she'd managed the buttons.

"I know what you mean," I said.

"Oh my dear. You must be beside yourself! I mean, she's just across the way from you, and then there's the issue of the brownies, I mean, how are you keeping it together?"

I thought Mrs. Gateway would hyperventilate on the spot. She was beginning to wheeze, making Grady glance about looking nervous.

"Let's just grab some dough, and get the heck out of here," he said.

The roar at the back of the room afforded us the distraction we needed to take advantage of the situation. Grady, Mrs. G. and I shot through the throng while all eyes were pointing to Bob.

"What? What?" he hollered. For a brief second we locked eyes, then he was off, doing what he did best. Most of the old folks were clapping or screaming with laughter. Bob had somehow managed to get one of April Fleet's voluminous skirts. It was bright purple, a color she wore in every shade, and he was doing a fine pirouette. The back zipper was undone to accommodate his expansive girth, although the fit wasn't too bad, and on the top he wore one of her frilly white blouses. If there was a question that it was hers, the nametag over his right nipple allayed any doubt. The silk material was like a second skin over his chest, and his arms looked like stuffed sausages. I thought he must be terribly uncomfortable, but it was an amazing sight.

"Oh ho!" Grady bellowed. "Here she comes!"

April, her face about the same shade as her purple skirt, elbowed her way through. She was positively sputtering, saying something about needing tighter security around the laundry room. What clinched it, though, was when Bob lifted his skirt and showed us a pair of flowered knickers. They were hugging his hips tighter than toddlers to their moms on the first day of kindergarten.

April gasped loudly and batted down the fabric. We didn't wait to see what was to come next. Bagels and Kaiser rolls in hand, Grady, Mrs. G. and I slipped the silvery bonds and were racing toward apartment 15, laughing so hard we could barely see.

Fanny was waiting for us when we got there, pacing and smacking a mouthful of blue gum.

"Well it's about time," she said, then spat the wad of gum into her hand and looked around for a trashcan. I could tell she'd had a restless night herself. She'd missed two pink curlers this time and they were waving around on the back of her head like newborn squirrels trying to nest.

"Bob's probably into the second act by now, but he'll be up soon," Grady said.

Ida stood there and it appeared as if she were trying to decide if she should play hostess or cohort. I felt a little bit sorry for her, since this obviously wasn't something she'd been anxious to be a part of, but that's just the way it is sometimes. We don't always get to pick our cards.

"I've got the hard drive ready to roll," Grady said to me. "You said you know someone who can help with this?"

"I'll give it a try."

"Give it a try?!" Fanny said. "We've only got one shot at this. You start asking around and it'll draw some questions, that's for sure. You've got to be right about this guy."

I shot a remark at Fanny. "You want to see what you can do?"

"Now girls. We're all bound to be jumpy. We don't have any choice. May, where is this person?"

"He works at the computer store. I think his name is Lance. At least it sounds right." I was making things up as I went along.

"May." Fanny was all business. I noticed her blue gum was poking out from behind one of her ears. "I was thinking last night, what if someone had tried to kill you? Don't you think it would be suspicious to see you out walking around?"

I hadn't thought of that, but I wasn't about to play dead. I'd just have to keep a low profile until this was all figured out. Was there anything else to complicate my life?

"And what about that first husband of yours? Maybe she got to him and he's got a family somewhere. That would be just the ticket, a prime motive for someone to want you gone." Fanny was making sense.

"We've got to get moving." Grady said. "Where the heck is Bob?"

"What? What?" Bob stuck his head through the door. He was out of April's clothes and oozing from a bikini. "Anyone for a swim?"

WE WORKED OUR WAY through the story first. I would be the one to call the police, saying I'd tried in vain to raise Mrs. Berkowitz with repeated knocks on her door. I would tell the police that I'd called my friends first in a panic, and they'd rushed right over. Bob would come in just after the police; provide some disturbance just to throw off their concentration. If they dusted for prints, vacuumed for fibers, or felt something was out of place I would just act like I was having a heart attack. But it wouldn't matter anyway, because being old and senile, none of us could possibly understand the importance of keeping a "crime scene" pristine and we would be bustling about touching things, knocking things over, messing things up. After all, we'd be in a great deal of shock. By that time, we'd planned to have the "clean" CPU back in place, the son would be called, and we'd have time to destroy all of the evidence once they were gone.

"It won't work," Fanny said, after we were all certain we had a foolproof way to be rid of the hauntings. "Her son will just pick up where she left off. Grady, even you said he's probably got copies of everything. We've got to come up with a way to stop him in his tracks."

We all felt like the wind had been snatched out of our sails. She was right, of course, darn the big-eyed lady.

"So, what's your idea?" Grady said. He put his hands over his face and rubbed at his stubble.

"We turn the tables. Find out what we can on him, then zap *him!*"

"Good Fanny. Really good. This guy's so low I doubt if he would even care," I said.

"There's got to be something. Some way," Ida said hopefully.

"Maybe there is, Grady," I said. "First let's get over to the computer store, see if this guy Lance can hack his way in to the CPU. Once we see what's there, we'll look around for anything. I don't know what, but something that we can use." It was a stretch but what did we have to lose?

"I'm ready whenever you are," Grady said, but he didn't look ready for anything. He looked like he needed a Tylenol. We took STUD DOC, after making sure most of the cronies were at the pool. Bob was standing on his hands at the midlevel, his feet were sticking out of the pool, and people were taking bets at how long he could hold his breath. Once clear of the gates, I stepped on the gas. Tina Turner was singing again, but I cut her off before she could be my private dancer.

"Grady, I know this is beside the point, but what are we going to do about the brownies? I mean, that may be the reason Mrs. Berkowitz is dead, it could have been me, and we don't know if any of this is related, or if I have a killer stalking me at this very minute."

"This is true and I've been working it over in my head. Did you know Fanny was once married to an LAPD detective?" So that explained her paranoia, or maybe it was just professional caution. She'd obviously learned a thing or two from her husband.

"She's bound to still have a few friend around who can help us. I'll bet she can get those crumbs analyzed."

"Why didn't she speak up then?" I was irritated again, waiting for a train both literally and figuratively, and not a little scared. "Maybe she didn't want to offer."

"What skeletons does she have hanging in her closet anyway? What did Mrs. Berkowitz have on her?"

"I guess you didn't read her spread sheet." Grady looked at me, studying me.

"No, what was it? Cheating at golf? Parking in a handicapped space illegally?"

"Nothing like that. She killed her husband."

I watched the trains blur in front of me, or maybe that was the way the whole world was beginning to look. "What? He interrupted her in the middle of Double Jeopardy?"

Grady pointed to the windshield. "Train's gone."

This was a story I'd have to hear from Fanny, and I could hardly wait. Since she didn't have bars on her windows I assumed she'd somehow beaten the rap. It must have been a juicy tidbit for our late Mrs. Berkowitz. Lance sighed heavily when he saw me push through the heavy double doors. I didn't hear him, but I could see his chest heaving, and knew he was looking around for a way out. I didn't let him get away.

"Excuse me!" I called over a long row of boxes. Lance looked left then right, but he was cornered. Sigh, sigh. "Yeah?"

That's yes ma'am, you impertinent little twerp. I got close enough to the pimple-faced teen to see the white centers of his acne. I could even smell the Stridex. He'd changed his hair color, this time to a mossy green. Could be he was getting moldy. I couldn't exactly tell. It happens if you don't shower enough. I got closer, and had to bend my head back a good bit. He was taller than I remembered.

"How good are you at this computer stuff?" I narrowed my eyes to a slit, giving him a challenge. If my guess was right, he was the kind of kid who spent all his spare time locked away in a dark room, peering into the bowels of a computer screen. He probably only socialized over the Internet and had virtual love affairs. I also gambled that he was proud of his abilities on the keyboard. I bated the hook, threw out the line, and he bit.

"I can do anything." His eyes narrowed to slits too, he and bent down, pushing his face closer to mine.

"Anything? Do you know about back doors? Can you hack in?" I'd learned a whole new language in the few hours I'd spent reading manuals and listening. It's what a writer does, I reminded myself, and what a good investigator does. You have to talk the talk when you're part of the underworld.

"I ain't never seen a code I couldn't break."

"Good! Good. How would you like to make a little cashola?" Reel him in.

Lance looked around again, then with a jerk of his head moved me in the direction of a quiet corner.

"How much we talkin'?"

Much too easy. "Can you call in sick tomorrow?"

"Am I not feeling well?"

"I'll triple whatever you make in a day here."

"Lady, I think I'm feeling a migraine coming on."

I gave Grady the high sign, but wouldn't answer any of his questioning looks until we were safely in my Camaro and down the road. I was feeling fine. I'd accomplished one mission, at least I'd gotten the ball rolling, and it appeared our Mr. Shish Kabob would be able to get us what we wanted. Then, that fine feeling sank low when I started thinking about it. We would have to put off the 911 call another day. By now Mrs. Berkowitz was probably drawing flies.

"Grady," I said, struck with the need for some fresh air and a little more time before heading home. Mind if we stop off at the park? I could use a walk about now."

"Thinking about those brownies," he said. It should have been a question, but he had been studying me. My husband always told me he knew what I was thinking before I opened my mouth. I guess I didn't hide my emotions very well.

"I still don't know why someone would want to kill me. Do you think it could be connected to what I found in Mrs. Berkowitz's apartment?"

"Why don't we grab a coffee and take that walk?"

Starbucks was on the way, and I got my usual Frappuccino, while Grady opted for the Mocha Grande. We walked around the crunchy pathways and talked easily.

"'S far as I can tell, you've got an enemy out there. You said your husband didn't have an axe to grind. Maybe he's afraid you'll go after him for money or something. Would he be capable of doing something like murder?" Grady sipped and grimaced.

"Wait 'til that cools or you'll burn your tongue off," I said. "My husband doesn't even know where I am. Besides, even if I got a huge settlement, that wouldn't put a dent in his money, and it wouldn't keep him from making a whole lot more in the future. I don't think I have to worry about him."

"What about your first husband?" Maybe he's remarried somewhere with a few kids and Mrs. Berkowitz's son tipped him off. He's trying to get you out of the way."

"It's possible, but I didn't even know he was still alive until recently." Then I stopped and looked at Grady as I remembered, "It makes my daughter illegitimate."

"More fuel for the fire." Grady appeared sickened by the thought. He genuinely looked sorry for me.

"She can never find out. Oh, Grady, we have to do something to put an end to all of this."

Grady took a deep breath and placed a hand on my shoulder. "We will May, whatever we have to do, whatever it takes. We'll take care of it."

Looking at him, his jaw set, his eyes unwavering, I believed him, and I trusted him. After all, he had as much to lose as the rest of us. Whatever we had to do.

THIRTEEN

WE GOT BACK TO the apartment and got the Clan together again. This time we sat on the balcony and each settled in with a Heineken before explaining our meeting with Lance. I had the boy's card in my wallet, and would call him first thing in the morning. I was curious about Fanny. She'd found time to redo her hair, and had put on a little makeup. As the light slowly slipped away and our conversation went round and round about what to do about Mrs. Berkowitz, her son, the files, my problem, we eventually got around to Fanny. What was her story?

She shifted uncomfortably at first when I gently questioned her about her life, but then her face fell, and I could tell she was ready to let go of the memories that had followed her all those years.

"My husband, George, was a detective with the LAPD," she began. I didn't let on that I'd heard of this, just leaned forward, silently encouraging her to continue. I glanced surreptitiously around the room and saw Ida was listening intently. I wondered if she knew anything about Fanny, and wondered how Grady had been privy to her past life. Bob was in his usual chair, straddle position, as quiet as a mouse. I didn't think he knew; he looked as captivated as I was. I urged her to go on.

"He liked to drink quite a bit, and it got worse when the pressures of work took their toll. He was very respected in his line of work, so I did my best to hide his drinking, but it was getting, well, out of hand." Fanny looked at her Heine and lifted it. "This would have been water to him."

The sprinklers kicked on, along with the automatic sidewalk lights. Our attention didn't waver, but it was hard to hear, so, reluctantly, we took a pause and moved the party indoors. Before Fanny started her story again, she put a finger to her lips. We all waited while she peeked under the phone, behind the curtains and in the flower vase, and ran her hands along the backs of the pictures on the wall.

"Bugs. Never can be too sure."

"I think we're okay, Fanny." Mrs. Gateway reassured her.

"Where was I?" Fanny said.

"Your husband was a lush," Bob said.

Mrs. Gateway frowned at him.

"Oh yes. Well, one night we were at this big party. It was at the commissioner's house, and everyone was there. A lot of important people. I was wearing a beautiful red chiffon, and had just gotten my nails done, French manicure, my hair was up in this roll on the back of my…"

"Fanny. The party?" Bob didn't care about her French manicure.

"Right. There were canapés, caviar, lots of wine and…well, a whole lot of drinking was going on, with my husband at the head of the pack."

"Six-pack," Bob mused.

"Right. No, I think it was more like Stolichnaya. Anyway. Will you just shut it and let me tell my story?"

"Sorry. Couldn't resist." Bob rubbed his nose.

"My husband was the life of the party. People were laughing and telling bad jokes, talking too much, getting loud. Before long, people were laughing *at* him because he was getting plowed and acting like a big horse's ass. I was embarrassed, furious really, so I got the car keys and told him we were leaving."

"Smart," Bob said. "Only friends let friends drive drunk. Something like that."

"Shut it, Bob." Ida said, and then blushed. "Sorry."

"I told him I was going to drive." Fanny looked at Ida, and then came back to me. "It made my husband so mad. He wore the pants in the family and I had just insulted his manhood, but I was just as angry and insisted we leave. The commissioner tried to intervene, he said we could stay overnight at his house, but the whole mess was just too humiliating, so I spun on my heel and headed for the driveway. I waited in the car for George to follow, which he did, staggering all the way."

Fanny handed Ida her empty bottle and took off her glasses. She rubbed at the lenses with angry, circular swipes. "I shouldn't have been so doggone stubborn. I should have let my husband sleep it off at the commissioner's house, but I had been drinking more than my share myself, and I wasn't thinking straight. I was just so angry."

"It happens," Mrs. G. said.

"When George got to the car he was practically having fits. He was going to drive that car, no matter what I did or said, and told me as much. Fine. I scooted over and handed him the keys. He was making such a spectacle. People were coming out of the house, and I didn't want a scene. He spun out of the driveway so fast, that he pelted the commissioner's pants with gravel."

"So embarrassing," Ida said.

"Hmm. Cops getting drunk and stoned," Bob said. "What next?"

"Shut up, Bob," I said.

"He drove like a madman. The car was all over the road and I was shouting at him to let me drive. When we were out of sight of the house, George calmed down a little and came to his senses. There wasn't anybody to impress anymore, and he knew he couldn't drive all the way home, so he pulled off the road and we changed places."

"So he let you drive after all," Bob said.

"It was dark, and I was tired. I just wanted to get home. I tried to ignore my husband 'cuz I was just so peeved, but he started making funny noises."

"Noises?" Ida looked around at the rest of us to explain. I shrugged my shoulders.

"George couldn't handle his liquor. Oh, he'd never admit to it, but he had the tolerance of a newt, and he'd had about six too many that night. I opened the window to let in some air. I turned on the radio. Nothing was working. George, was about to, about to, um…"

"Blow chunks," Bob nodded. "I've seen it."

"We had this brand new car. It still had that new car smell and everything. I'll have to admit I wasn't feeling very sympathetic, I was still pretty ticked, and I'd had more than my share of wine that night. I threatened him. Told him he'd better not get sick in the car, to roll down the window and stick his head out. I was shoving at him, telling him to hurry up. Guess I wasn't watching the road very well at that point, myself." Fanny paused for a minute, looking at each of us in turn.

"So he stuck his head out the window. It was right in front of the Petersons' house. They had this really big mailbox, and, well, I was just a little too close."

"Too close?" Ida wasn't getting it.

"You know, close, close!" Fanny held her hands about an inch apart. We got the idea. "He leaned out, all the way up to his shoulders, and, whack! He bounced his head off that mailbox. Made a really big dent, too."

"Oh, Fanny, what did you do?" I asked.

"Luckily the Petersons were out of town. They didn't hear a thing that night, and after I picked up their mail—it was all over the road, I stood by the car just looking at my husband. He was still hanging out the open window from the waist down, mouth open, blood dripping onto the pavement. The flashers on my car were going and it would only be a few minutes before the rest of the party started driving by. We were going to attract some attention."

"Was he…?" Ida couldn't finish.

"Didn't feel a thing. Dead as yesterday," Fanny said. "I had to act fast. Cars would be coming along any minute, and I was the one driving when George mailed his last letter. I'd been drinking too. If the cops did a blood test, I would have been put in jail for manslaughter. I would have been there a long time. The laws weren't as forgiving as they are now."

"It was an accident though," Ida said.

"I went a little crazy. Remember, I was pretty looped, and there was George dangling, bleeding, so I did what I had to do."

We all leaned forward.

"I got back into the car, threw it into reverse and backed down the road. Then I aimed for the mailbox a second time, only when I hit it again I plowed over it, bounced off the road, down into the barrow pit and slammed the car against a telephone pole."

"Oh my gosh, Fanny!" Ida said.

"Could have been stupid. I could have killed myself, but I came away with a gash on the forehead and a sprained ankle. Not too bad. Then I saw some lights coming down the road and I panicked. How I did it I still don't know. I just grabbed my husband, and shoved him toward the steering wheel. I crawled over his body and waited for the lights to get close enough. Then I barreled out the passenger side and stood there screaming and waving."

I could see the image so clearly and imagined Fanny, a young beauty in her pretty red chiffon, now covered in blood, her husband dead behind the wheel of their car. It must have been sheer horror.

"The cops came, a few of them were from the party. They had seen my husband get in the car stone drunk, and there was never a question that I had been an innocent passenger. I let them believe this, and I watched as my husband was lowered into the ground knowing I'd been the one who put him there. I vowed to live with that secret the rest of my life. Until Mrs. Berkowitz sent me a letter. There was even a newspaper clipping of the accident. And you know what else?"

"What Fanny?" Grady asked.

"A little bundle of letters. The Petersons' letters! I'd shoved them in my glove box after the accident and lost them when the car was towed away."

"How in the world?" Bob asked. He threw his arms up and I thought he was going to shout out, "What? What?" But he didn't. He'd just said what we were all thinking.

"I don't know," Fanny said quietly. She replaced her

glasses but they were fogging. She ran withered fingers over them leaving smudges.

"Did you tell anyone about this?" I asked, trying to probe her memory.

"I went to a psychiatrist after that; I was barely holding myself together. The trauma had nearly immobilized me. He gave me some medication, and I talked with him for about six months until I was able to get through it all."

"And you spilled everything," Bob said.

"But it was all confidential! Medical ethics, you know?" Fanny looked hurt.

"That woman's evil knew no bounds." Grady said. He thumped his fist into his other palm. "Prying into psych records? Medical records? Marriage licenses? Her son must be one busy S.O.B."

"The price must be right," I answered. "There must be a lot of money in extortion."

"If you think about it, you get a little out of a lot of people and soon you can be vacationing on the French Riviera every weekend," Grady said.

"On your own yacht," Bob said.

"Flying over in your private jet," Ida said.

"When will it be over?" Fanny looked older then, if it was possible. She had crumpled into her chair like a wet rag.

"We'll know something tomorrow." I upended my bottle and drained the last of it. Let's get some sleep and meet again in the morning."

"I'll save us a table down by the pool," Bob said, standing. He scooted his chair away and it made a scree sound on the kitchenette linoleum. "Come on May, I'll walk you back."

We were nearing the balcony of the plant man when Mr. Greenjeans suddenly stepped out of the shadows. I gasped loudly, about to thump him with my purse, when Bob stepped forward and shouted into his face, "What? What?" Mr. Greenjeans scuttled away, nearly dropping a coil of hose hanging off his shoulder.

"Doesn't he ever sleep?" Bob glowered, watching until the handyman disappeared around the corner of the building. I could smell faint traces of oil and dirt following in Mr. Greenjeans' wake.

"I doubt it, after that scare you gave him."

"He's always lurking. Have you noticed? He seems to be everywhere."

"You're starting to sound paranoid," I said.

"Aren't you feeling it? Like people aren't really who they are? I mean, like everyone around here is wearing a mask, and if you peeled away the outer layer, underneath would be someone entirely different?"

"Bob. Take a look in the mirror."

"I've got my reasons." Bob caught my smile and answered it with a broad grin, although it didn't go beyond his mouth.

"Bob. We know about Fanny and about Grady, but what did Mrs. Berkowitz have on you?"

"On crazy Bob?" Bob ran his hand around on his belly as we walked. "That's a long story. It'll keep 'til tomorrow."

"Probably better than Mrs. Berkowitz," I said.

FOURTEEN

THAT NIGHT I HAD dreams of Fanny standing at the side of the road. She was in her red dress, but the fabric wasn't chiffon, it was made of Peel and Pull licorice strings. She was sorting mail, saying "Ed McMahon! Lookie here, Georgie Porgy. We've won a million dollars!" Her face changed, and she was Mrs. Berkowitz, cackling and reaching out to grab my collar; then she changed again, and it was Grady sitting in a smoke-filled room holding a hand full of aces. On his nose were rubbery black sunglasses that dripped inky stains onto his white banker shirt. The cards started moving and Ida stood up behind them, her hands scissoring in a blur as she knitted a potholder. "Want some cookies? Want some cookies? Want some brownies?" she asked with breathless urgency. Bob appeared and reached out to take the ticking needles from her hand but the needles turned into loops of hose and wrapped around the arms of Mr. Greenjeans. *"I told you to leave it alone. I told you to stay clear!"* Mr. Greenjeans disappeared, and it was Mr. Ramirez holding Paco by the tail. "Yap, yap, yap!" Paco went on and on. I threw my hands over my ears and then I woke up.

'Yap, yap, yap!' Paco had begun his morning wake up call and I was never happier to hear the little rat. I was dressing in a hurry when I heard something that was more alarming than a bump in the night.

"Mrs. Berkowitz! Yoo-hoo! Mrs. Berkowitz!" I scurried to the door and took my customary position at the peephole. The greater part of the landing was taken up by April's expansive skirt, the one that had adorned Bob's figure just yesterday. (Hoped she'd washed it at least.) She tapped impatiently at the door opposite mine. Her door. She reached for the knob. Had we locked it?

I got the chain off my door in such a rush of hyper-activity that I chipped two nails.

"April, hi." I tried to sound casual but my voice warbled like a wren. April released the knob, and turned, somewhat surprised. That was close.

"Oh, hello Mrs. List, is everything okay? I've been trying to raise Mrs. Berkowitz but she's not answering her door." April had the look of a concerned parent.

"She's not there," I said a bit too quickly. "I mean, I think I heard her earlier, so she must have been there, but she's not there now. She's probably down at the pool."

Get away from that door! "That's funny." April frowned harder. "She doesn't go to the pool." Then the lavender-clad woman put her hand next to her mouth and whispered, "She's a shut-in."

"Maybe she's in the shower. I'll tell you what. I can

pass on a message if you'd like." *Get away from the cotton pickin' door!*

"I suppose that'll be okay. It's you I want to talk to anyway." April fiddled with a string of beads around her neck. I let my breath out a little.

"Me?" My voice sounded squeaky.

"You were saying how uncomfortable your apartment is, and Mrs. Berkowitz is coming to the end of her lease. I thought you might want to switch over to her apartment. It always seems to be a bit cooler."

Oh yes, like a morgue. "That would be nice," I lied.

"I was just about to ask Mrs. Berkowitz if she wouldn't mind letting you take a look, to see if it was suitable for you."

"I can certainly give her the message. In fact—" I was moving April toward the stairs gently, my hand on her elbow. *Was that the same blouse Bob had on yesterday?* "—I'll just take a look myself when she gets out of the shower. I'm sure she won't mind. I'll let you know." I was practically pushing her down the stairs now. If I got my feet behind her, she'd probably bounce just like my typewriter.

"Very well then, you just let me know what you think." April was moving off, on her own now, and I stood at the top of the landing, waving. She turned for a minute, her hand clutching her necklace, mouth open, as if she were about to say something else.

"I'll let you know," I said, with as much merriment as I could muster.

"Have a good day, Mrs. List, I hope this works out for you."

You and me both, I thought, and waved my little hand off.

Crap! I thought, when she was halfway down the walk. Too close. I watched her a little bit longer as she had stopped to tell Mr. Greenjeans something, pointing at the carport beams, then moved off, her wide, purple bottom pumping left, right, left, right. I had to see if we'd locked the door. I reached my hand out to the knob then stopped just short of touching it. I reached in my pocket and found a tissue. No sense leaving prints. The knob turned easily and, once again, I was staring into Mrs. Berkowitz's apartment. A cool breeze hit me square in the face, along with the pungent smell of Oil of Olay and something a bit more cloying.

I slammed the door shut. *Crap! Who forgot to lock the door?* Of course, no one had locked the door, because no one had her keys. This only meant one thing. I was going to have to go back into the crypt and find her keys. Now that would be a story to tell when the 911 guys came and found her apartment locked and no sign of keys. How would I explain that one? I really needed the advice of the group and I *really* didn't want to go back in there alone.

I got Bob on the phone and explained my dilemma. He started laughing, but I'm sure it was more nerves than hilarity when I told him about the apartment manager.

"Wait right there. I'm coming up," he said.

Less than a minute later, Bob was at my door.

"What is *that?*" I asked him after checking to see if he'd been followed. He was wearing a Hawaiian grass skirt. It was covered partially by his drooping tummy. On his chest rustled a large lei, made I presumed, by some of the flowers from around the complex. I could still smell the scent of lavender. His feet were bare.

"Sometimes I like to wear something that makes me feel utterly feminine."

"Therapy, Bob."

"I tried that. I think my shrink committed suicide." Bob turned serious for a minute. "That manager can actually be our savior," he said. "She's got a master key and I know where it is. All I have to do is work a bit of my magic."

"You're going to steal her keys?"

"Only for a little while until we can make a copy. Then, voila! We lock the door from the outside and no one's the wiser."

"I don't know how long I can hold her off." I brushed the hair away from my face and came away with a few strands. "Look. I'm losing my hair. I don't think I can keep this up."

"I know where I can get a good wig—cheap," Bob said. His eyes were twinkling.

"Ugh." I cringed. "Just get the key. I have an appointment with a computer nerd."

Lance showed up right on time. At least he was prompt, if nothing else. I gave him the song and dance about being given a computer hard drive, but had turned it over to a friend who couldn't get into it because of the passwords. He looked at me with that bored, faraway look I'd seen in the faces of too many teenagers lately, but this time I figured it was an advantage. I didn't want him to be too curious. I steered him around the complex toward Grady's place. Ida, Grady and Fanny met us there. They were dressed in flip-flops, wide hats, and sunscreen, on their way to the pool. I made brief introductions, then offered Lance a chair (I learned his name was really Brad, but I had a hard time making that transition, especially when I saw another metal object pierced through his tongue.)

"You just take your time. I don't figure you want a bunch of old folks looking over your shoulder." Fanny and Ida giggled innocently, just a couple of nice old ladies curious about the workings of a newfangled machine. Nice touch, girls.

Lance grunted, and held out a hand. I took it gently in mine. He was polite after all. He sighed.

"Oh. You need your cashola." I raised an eyebrow to Grady who fished in his pocket.

"Two hundred now, two hundred when you finish." Grady the banker.

"Right." Lance tucked the bills into the brim of his baseball hat, pushed his hair back, and replaced the hat backwards on his head.

"You know they make those brims for a reason," Grady started, but I quieted him with a quick shake of my head. We didn't need a grandfatherly lecture at the moment.

"How much time do you think you'll need, dear?" Ida was oozing sugar, while her hands were twisting the handles of her beach bag into nervous knots.

"Give me an hour. If I'm not done by then, it can't be done." Lance was already clicking away, so we gave him a pat, and backed out the door. "What do you think?" Grady pulled chairs around an umbrella table at the south end of the pool. It was early, so we were alone. Even Mr. Greenjeans hadn't shown up to sweep the pool yet. Ida set a picnic basket on the table and started lifting out croissants, rolls, jellies, fruit and a carafe of coffee. I stared at the basket, drooling. I couldn't remember the last time I'd had anything to eat, and I was about to start chewing on the wicker if someone didn't hand over a banana pretty soon.

"He seems to know what he's doing," Fanny said, pushing the walker away before she reached for the coffee cups. She poured, and I added cream to my cup. At least I'd get my calcium. That cup of coffee was the best I'd ever had, and the croissants were heavenly. I made two disappear before posing my question to Fanny.

"Do you know anyone in police business anymore?" I wanted to sound casual. Fanny was trying to chew around her teeth, which kept disengaging from her gums. She had a dollop of blueberry jam on her chin. "I mean, have you kept in touch with any of your old friends?" I handed her a napkin.

"They can't help us with this," Ida said. Grady shot me a look. He knew where I was going.

"That's not what I mean. Somebody has to get the brownie crumbs to a lab for analysis. We need someone who won't ask a lot of questions, someone who we can confide in. Do you know anybody Fanny?"

"Like at a crime lab? Forensics?" Fanny seemed to be searching her memory.

"Yes! They don't even have to be from around here. We can overnight the baggie, and ask for an analysis by phone. I've thought about it. We just say my cat got into the garbage, ate some of this stuff and died. Innocent."

"And what if it turns out there is something in the brownies? What then?" Ida asked.

"Then at least we'll know how Mrs. Berkowitz died," I said.

"And you'll know you've got bigger problems than you ever imagined." Leave it up to Fanny to put things into perspective.

"I'm sure it was just an accident," Ida said very quietly, absently pushing butter around on a bite of biscuit. I couldn't see her face under the wide hat, but she sounded genuinely troubled. Poor Ida. It couldn't be easy to admit the possibility of malfeasance in a perfect world of potholders and Depends, much less find yourself in the middle of it all.

"Okay. There's this guy who used to chase me around a few years after my husband died. He played the field quite a bit, had a reputation around the precinct where my husband worked. I never took him seriously, but for a while he was ruthless. He really went all out to get my attention. We did a lot of things together, but there was no, well, what do you call it?"

"Chemistry?" Ida said. Good. She was coming around. Love was a much safer topic than murder.

"Right. No chemistry. I think I broke his heart, but it didn't stop him from trying for years. Eventually I moved away, he got married, had a few kids and I lost touch. I'm sure he's retired, maybe even dead. But as far as I know he never left the area, and could probably find a way to get those crumbs analyzed if he's still breathing."

"He's the kind of guy who carries a torch?"

"Blazing."

"Okay Fanny, we need all the charm you can muster. You up to it?" Grady asked.

"Say no more. This old gal hasn't completely lost it."

Fanny's mouth curved into a smile, and for a minute I saw her wrinkles smooth away; I could imagine how lovely and beautiful she'd been at one time. She could do this.

"We have to move quickly." Grady brought me back to the present. "May, you get the goodies, I'll go check on our friend at the computer. Fanny, you get on the phone. If you're nervous, use the pay phone over at the market. Ida, you go with Fanny. Everyone ready?"

We sat poised, like a platoon of soldiers ready to take the hill. "Break!" Grady said, and slapped his hands together. Fanny shuffled off behind her walker as fast as her tiny feet could go. Ida hustled along behind her, Grady grabbed the picnic basket and I grabbed a banana. Then I flew back to my apartment.

It was impossible to avoid Mr. Ramirez as I bounced up the steps. "May! May List!"

Paco was being impertinent. He'd tipped off the Mariachi man. Maybe he'd like a few brownie crumbs before they went off to the lab. I paused, plastered a pleasant look on my face then slowly backed down the steps.

"Yes Mr. Ramirez?" I noticed a new collection of gadgets on his "workbench." How could he even move about his porch with all of that stuff?

"Check out my new invention." Mr. Ramirez was sporting some sort of metal hat. With a flip of his finger he pushed a welder's mask over his face and bent into a display of glass, paper and wood fragments on his bench. Something clicked and a flame shot out of a canister in his hand. I recognized it as a welding torch. He had that sucker up full flame. It hissed and licked at the bottom of a glass tube filled with a clear liquid. A loud boom shook the floor, the workbench, my constitution, and knocked Mr. Ramirez back through his screen door. When the smoke cleared, Mr. Ramirez emerged, his metal hat sitting sideways on his head, his face covered in soot.

"Guess I didn't have the calculations set right." He looked a bit frazzled, but not too concerned. "Was supposed to go up like an Estees Rocket. My new paper delivery system." A shower of newspaper fell like confetti, snowing down over both of us.

"I'm sure you'll get it right next time," I assured him, and brushed the snow out of my hair. "You just keep at it."

"Right. Right." Mr. Ramirez was lost in his own thoughts, and I took the moment to get away. It was nearing the bottom of the hour and I had to find out what was going on at Grady's place. The brownie crumbs found their way into my purse, and I was back out the door and past Mr. Ramirez before he could shine his tooth my way.

FIFTEEN

"HOLY MERCIFUL MOTHER!" I heard Grady exclaim
when I slipped into his living room. He was pacing,
dragging a long stream of paper. He didn't even notice
me until I put my hand on his arm.

"What is it?" I asked, glancing nervously at the
door. Ida had snuck in behind me.

"Close the door. And draw the curtains too while
you're at it." I didn't have time to be civil or polite, I
was worried that Grady was a smidgen too loud. Ida
did as she was told, glancing back at Grady, wondering, as I was, what the papers were telling him.

"I think I've got everything." Lance walked out of
the bedroom and I could tell it hadn't been an easy assignment. His multi-colored hair was wet around the
hatband, and his face was slick and ruddy. But he'd
been successful.

"Yes. Thank you." Grady dug the rest of the money
out of his pocket and waved it at the boy without taking
his eyes off of the paper. "I assume you understand this
is, um, confidential?" I was trying to get an idea of
what the boy might be thinking but his face was un-

readable. His expression changed somewhat as he folded the bills into his hand.

"I know, I was never here, never stopped by, been in bed all day."

"Thank you." I caught his eyes then, and I knew I'd found a trusted friend. I waited until I heard his car door slam before grabbing Grady's arm again. I was dying to get a look at those printouts."

"Ladies, you might as well sit. This is bigger than I ever imagined," Grady said.

"Wait," I said. "Where's Fanny?"

"She's still at the phone. I had to get her about ten rolls of quarters," Ida said.

"Shouldn't we wait for her?" I asked.

"She'll know soon enough." Grady started folding up the paper carefully, end over end, until it was nearly as thick as an encyclopedia. One side was covered with ink, row after row of *data*. So much *data!* Even as I tried to make sense of it all, the printer continued to chug away in the other room.

"It's still going?" I asked Grady.

"This is just a start. I got a look at the file, and someone's gonna have to make a paper and ink run before it's all done. I just hope my old printer can handle the job. It's slow, but it really doesn't matter. It will give us time to go over everything as it prints out."

Grady kept shaking his head as he scanned the pages. He made room on his table and signaled Ida and me over. "It's all here." I looked over Grady's shoulder,

Ida slipped into a chair and put her elbows on the table, Grady couldn't stop shaking his head. We were at the bottom of the fifth page when Fanny's walker clattered outside the door. Grady hustled to let her in.

"I found him! I can't believe I found him! He's agreed to take the crumbs over to the lab. His friend still works there, an old friend who knows how to keep his mouth shut." Fanny looked flushed but excited. And happy. "He's widowed, and unofficially retired, but he serves as a court expert witness now. It sounds so exciting! I just knew he would help."

I handed her my purse with the Ziploc inside and went back to the printout. "What did you find?"

Fanny stood behind me to get a peek. Then she whistled long and low (although it sounded a bit like a tire losing air around those new teeth of hers). "I had no idea," she said.

"It must have taken years to get all of this," Grady said. "Bank account numbers, personal holdings, stocks, bonds, credit cards, mothers' maiden names, all current."

"Account withdrawals, transfers, shares in stock, investments, this stuff goes way back too." I didn't know much about the intricacies of the business world, but I knew about money, and there were dollar signs everywhere. Lots of dollar signs.

"She's certainly been busy," Ida said scornfully.

"There's enough information here to give her access to these people's identity, to siphon off their savings without anyone knowing, transfer funds, skim a little here and a little there, invest with their money and replace it before they're the wiser." Grady sounded both angry and awed by the whole scheme. I doubt even in his banking life he'd seen anything close to this magnitude of larceny. It was nearly impossible to imagine.

"I'm sure that's just what she's been doing," I added. "The little money she's been collecting with their permission is just the tip of the iceberg."

"So many people!" Fanny was erupting. "What are we going to do about it?"

"Grady, you were in banking a long time. Have you ever run across anything like this before?"

"I probably wouldn't have known if I had. Since Mrs. Berkowitz hasn't been caught, it's probably been so well laundered that nobody has noticed any misappropriations. There are wire transfers and phone transfers all the time. If you have certain personal details, account numbers, and forged signatures, it's really not that hard. The thing that makes this different is that nobody has brought it to the attention of the authorities. If there had been one hint, there would have been an investigation, and eventually the pieces would have come together. They would have followed the trail back to Mrs. B. But nobody was about to do that. In fact, the people on this list would have done whatever they could to *avoid* an investigation."

"She knew too much about everyone, and she knew they would never talk," Ida said. "Anything to avoid an upset."

"And everyone was our age," Fanny said.

"Old," I said, although I didn't feel old. I looked at the birth dates following the names of all of those people, and some were younger than me. We were all in our twilight years, happy to ride out our days without hassle or disruption. The perfect targets.

"I don't mind a little upset." I said aloud. Boy, was that the understatement of the year. I'd turned my whole world upside down in a few short days. What's another wrench in the cogs of my life?

"What?" Fanny was tucking the Ziploc into a little cloth bag hanging on the handle of her walker.

"We've got to get this money back where it belongs. It might take us all night, but we have to come up with some plan to return the money. Can we do that Grady?"

"This is going to take some thinking. We'll have to find out where Mrs. Berkowitz was stashing the money. So far, I've seen several accounts where the money was transferred to, and I'll bet it isn't going into the benevolent society of Shriners. In fact, it's out of the country."

"We'll just take it one person at a time, pull it from her account, then put it back into theirs."

"How are we going to do that?" Fanny looked incredulous.

"I think I have a way." Grady was smiling. "May, you're about Mrs. Berkowitz's size, aren't you?" He was giving me an appraising look, craning his neck.

"What? Me?" I laughed. "She's about half my size!"

"No, dear, you're really close," Ida said. She was giving me the once-over, making me feel like a circus sideshow. "Within ten pounds or so, I'd say."

"I don't think so." I felt embarrassed. But then I had been on a pretty strict diet of raw nerves and adrenaline lately, not to mention the added little bit of exercise.

"Just a minute." I slipped into Grady's bathroom and stepped onto the small white scale I'd seen there earlier. I gasped as the needle hovered ten pounds below the usual. When I came back into the room, I had to agree. "Pretty close." And whatever Grady had planned, it would be fine, because I was ten pounds lighter. Look out Bambie, May Bell's takin' over.

We were all anxious to put our plan into action but it was time for exercise class, and Bob showed up at my apartment to act as an escort. He still wore his ridiculous outfit, although the grass in his skirt was sparser than before. We secured Mrs. Berkowitz's place, at least for the time being. He told me he had kept April close, in order to head her off if she tried another surprise visit; in fact, he'd kept her master key just in case.

"Think we should check on her?" Bob asked. He twirled the key ring around his index finger.

"We can't," I said quickly. "We'll be late for class if we do." The last thing I wanted was to take a peek at the little extortionist "napping" on her couch. "Besides, someone might see us coming out of her apartment."

"Gives you the creeps, huh."

"She isn't going anywhere." I was trying to be strong.

"Did you ever think maybe she's not dead?" Bob gave me the impression he enjoyed watching me cringe. I heard his grass skirt rustle and it wasn't because of any breeze blowing through; he had an itch. Well, who could blame him, with all that tickling, dried grass? I was developing a few itches myself, hives probably, and I'd even noticed one of my eyelids was dancing slightly.

"It's getting really hot." I rubbed my neck and came away with a wet palm. "It might be a problem." Bob understood when I waved my hand in front of my nose, casting a look toward Apartment 3C. "But I don't suppose we can do anything about it." More rustling, Bob was busy with one hand; with the other he stroked his chins.

"If the smell starts getting bad, it might alert someone. We've got to get some fans in there."

"Before I could stop him, Bob was yanking the cords out of my new box fans, and had one under each arm on his way out the door before I grabbed the back of his grass skirt and hauled him back. "Wait a minute! We'll be late for exercise class!"

"Right!" Bob lowered the fans to the floor. He threw the lei over one beefy shoulder and snapped his fingers. "Right! Another hour won't matter much, but all the same, I think it would be a good idea if I cut the class a little short." Bob adjusted his skirt and rustled out the door. I glanced at my watch. Just enough time to find my sweats. Bob was going to cut the class short? I couldn't help but think to myself, *best leid plans…*

SIXTEEN

SOMETHING WAS DIFFERENT at the Active Senior health spa. The Center had been transformed into a homeless shelter. There were little blue mattresses all over the floor, and withered transients in caustic-colored Lycra were napping on the thin foam cushions.

"Howdy, Ma'am!" Mr. Scissorhands stood by a pile of the mats wearing camouflaged shorts, and an olive drab T with the words *Semper Fi* embossed in gold across the front. His legs were stork-like, allowing lots of air to scoot up through the legs of his shorts. "Aaaa Yaaa!" The old Marine had just stormed Normandy. He took a defensive stance, crouching low, both hands slicing the air. Then he kicked one leg out, spun around rapidly, and smacked a blue cushion from the top of the pile. The mat skittered across the floor and came to rest near Fanny's walker.

"Dadnabbit Fred!" Fanny hefted her walker and started stabbing dents in Fred's mat. I hurried over before Fanny gave herself away. So much for feeble/disabled.

"Now, now. He's just practicing his Judo. No harm done. Fiddle dee dee." I gave Fanny the eye and slid Mr. Scissorhands back to the next row.

"Ten months in the bush. I could knock a pith helmet off a guy's head with this leg and be gone before he could shout, 'Oh my Seoul!'" Fred gave his thin thigh a whack and I noticed a pink handprint starting to form. That must have hurt.

"May. Get yourself a mat over there. It's floor time today." Mrs. Gateway was at my elbow, hurrying me along. The torture queen had just made her way onto the platform, calling the shelter to order with her whistle.

Floor time? I saw the masses begin to worm their way around on the mats, heard a lot of grunting and popping, and pathetic attempts at putting legs into what should have been the lotus position. Limbs of every size were wrapped, bent and pulled in every direction. Someone in the front managed briefly, then fell over face first. I heard a soft thud, but she was up in a second, saying quietly, "I'm okay, I'm okay."

I got my mat on the floor, got my seat down on the cold blue vinyl and got my legs bending, but the nearest thing I could get to the lotus was to put my heels together and hold onto my calves. That would have to do. Mrs. Gateway was huffing off to my right, but Fanny was a pretzel, showing off a bit by touching her toes to her ears.

"Knock it off!" I hissed at the old lady. She looked at me with the biggest, brightest eyes and locked her ankles in place on her shoulders.

"I can roll over on my back like this and play a little beat on my bum if you want!" Fanny chuckled.

"Fanny!" I looked around, but everyone was more interested in his or her own gyrations, and besides, the warden was tweeting again.

"Oh alright, killjoy." Fanny unwrapped herself and sat hunched, rubbing her joints. Better.

"Now bend!"

My toes were out there somewhere, like little nubs on the horizon, but if I leaned forward, reaching, reaching, maybe they would come to me. Why were my feet moving away?

"Gooooood!" purred the matron. She was wearing a new outfit this time, I suppose it was her floor work getup, blue skin-tight cotton shorts topped by a thin strapped shirt to match, equally restraining, and buffering in all the right places. Nothing was a-sway on this lady. She even had the temerity to wear a delicate gold chain around her waist, as if to show us all that sweat and dislocated shoulders can also be fashionable. Her ponytail had a life of its own, spanking her head with each bob and weave. I'd like to give her a bob and weave.

"Now place your head on the mat in front of you and don't forget to breeeeeathe!"

Fanny flopped forward; I could hear her snuffing heavily into the blue foam. Mrs. Gateway was turning beet red, tiny veins popping like blue rivers along her temples, giving it her best, while I just worked to keep my waistband from disappearing into my belly rolls. I kept one covert eye on the activity toward the front of the room.

There he was. Behind a velvet curtain off to the side I saw Bob; he hadn't changed from his outfit in the interest of time. I couldn't believe a man that size could move as quickly as he did, but before the cluster of blue haired writhers could utter their usual fore-warning, Bob darted toward the torture queen, and dropped down behind her. When she stood to give us our next assignment, Bob shot between her legs and grabbed her ankles, knocking her off balance. His grass skirt had parted at his massive thighs, giving us a glimpse at the rounded parts nobody should see. There was a blessed slip of lawn hanging down between the mountains, and I was glad we weren't witness to the eye of the needle at any rate. When Bob got to his feet, the ponytailed drill sergeant was riding his bare shoulders, her feet tangled in the withered lei. She was gasping and flailing, her mouth a quivering "O," and Bob faced the applauding group shouting, "What? What?"

That tore it. I gathered my mat and had it tossed into a corner before April could break up the show. Fanny took my cue and clattered along behind me, Mrs. Gateway was quick on our heels. The whole center was in a furor. Blue mats flew through the air like a ticker tape parade; towels were swinging, and Mr. Scissor-hands got his shears on the boom box. Out the door we went, pushed along by the thumping rhythm of INXS singing "New Sensation."

We hotfooted it back to Ida's apartment, Fanny's

aluminum walker striking the sidewalk every third step or so.

"Where's Grady?" I asked Ida when we were in front of Fernon's balcony. He was pruning his philodendrons with a pair of pinking shears. Plastic snippets were shooting out onto the lawn and his ivy looked practically naked.

"Looks like rain!" he said, and stuck a scrawny hand out over the balcony rail. I caught sight of a cat on the balcony above his. Its yellow eyes were gleaming. "I don't think it'll last long," I called out cheerfully. "Just a little tinkle."

"Yeah, get a lot of those. A shower and it's over. Good for the plants anyway!" Nice old man.

"Grady said he had an idea." Ida huffed along. "He told me to cover for him at the exercise class. You know—if April started asking questions." Her long cotton shorts were giving her fits. They were wrapping around her thighs, bunching around her Depends. She looked both ways and plucked at the back of them with two fingers.

Fanny was already at Ida's door, giving us a "hurry up" look. The phone was ringing in Ida's apartment while we tumbled over each other trying to get the door closed behind us. Ida snatched up the receiver, said hello, then just stood there saying nothing. Fanny and I leaned in, heard a male voice on the phone, but couldn't make out any of the words. Ida looked at us, perplexed.

"Who is it?" Fanny mouthed.

Ida put her hand over the phone, looking more concerned than ever, and whispered, "It's Grady, but I can't understand a thing he's saying. It's all gibberish."

Fanny grabbed the phone out of Ida's hand. "It's got to be code. Here." I leaned in closer. "Ummhmm. Yes. Right. Ten-four. Roger. Wilco. O and O." Fanny replaced the receiver and looked at us smugly."

"What was he saying?" Ida had her fingertips to her mouth. Her fingernails were looking a little ragged. The pink polish was chipping in places. Yep, life in the underworld will do that to a person.

"'*Get the chickens to the coop.*' Means that we're all supposed to go over to Mrs. Berkowitz's place. '*The fox got away from the hounds.*' Means Bob escaped from April and is probably already at the coop right now. Didn't you ever watch 'Mission Impossible'? Sheesh." Ida looked hurt, Fanny looked proud of herself, and I just thought it was all too loony for words.

"Ida, are you sure that's what he meant? Maybe he wants us to go to his place, or mine, or maybe it was something else altogether." The last thing I wanted to do was go back over to that old lady's apartment. Grady and Bob could put her darned computer back and leave us out of it. Heck no, I won't go.

My hesitation must have shown. Fanny gave the back of my head a swat. "Come on girlie, get some giblets. She can't hurt you now."

"It's just that I haven't eaten anything all day. I'm

feeling a little weak and shaky. Why don't you two go and I'll drive on over to Subway and get us some sandwiches."

Fanny swatted the back of my head a second time.

"Stop that!" I smoothed my hair down. The little trickles were starting down my front again and my upper lip was getting moist.

"Have you forgotten that you were the one with the brownies?" Fanny may as well have smacked me between the eyes that time.

"Alright. Let's just get this over with."

Grady must have been watching. He had the door open and waved us in the minute we reached the top of the landing. Bob was arranging my box fans around the couch.

"How did you get those?" I kept my eyes away from the thing under the blanket.

Bob jingled the keys. "Forgot I had these? Hope you don't mind, but I took your last Evian. You need to do some grocery shopping anyway; your fridge looks like a wasteland."

"That's none of your business," I said.

"She doesn't look too bad," Fanny was saying. "A little blue, her teeth are starting to show, but other than that, she's held up pretty good, I'd say."

I looked at Ida, and she looked at me, and it was impossible not to look at Fanny who was bent over the couch, her white tousled head doing an examination of our beloved Mrs. Berkowitz.

"Come on. See for yourself." Fanny stepped aside.

Cautiously, I made my way to the afghan. She was right. Mrs. Berkowitz hadn't done too badly. Her gums were pretty blue, and they had drawn back a bit in a yellow-toothed grin, her eyes were still closed and sunken slightly, her cheeks were drawn, but other than that, her skin wasn't peeling or anything, and the only bad smell was her thick coating of Oil of Olay. Maybe I should get some of that. It worked as a pretty good preservative. Bob got the fans billowing. They were so noisy it was impossible to talk quietly in her living room, so we crowded into her computer center. Grady had somehow gotten her hard drive back on her desk and was attaching wires and cords. He had to go under the desk for the last attachments, and his pants pulled down making any plumber jealous. Mrs. Gateway blushed and looked away.

"There! Got it." Grady popped up, his face matching Ida's crimson. He got to his feet. I waited… then…yes, one thumb.

I let out my breath. "It's all back like it was?" I asked.

"With only a few minor adjustments." Grady smiled broadly. "Lucky for us, Mrs. Berkowitz was tidy, if nothing else. No dust to worry about."

"You're not wearing gloves," Fanny was scowling. "Where are your gloves?"

"Oops," Grady said.

"Oops? Oops? Now we'll have to wipe everything

down. More fibers, more evidence. Sheesh, Grade." Fanny hurried off to find a towel.

Ida put a hand on Grady's arm in a soothing manner. "You did real good Grady. I'm so proud of you."

Grady beamed and patted Ida's hand. "Does that mean you're ready to give the Viagra a whirl?" he asked.

"Not with a man who feeds my cookies to the birds." It was Grady's turn to blush.

"Hey you two—get a room. But later. Right now I want to know why you called us all back up here. It's going to get a little bit suspicious if people notice us coming in and out of this apartment." I had my hands on my hips. Besides, I was starving. The exercise class took it out of me. So much stretching.

"I think I've found out where Mrs. Berkowitz was squirreling away her money. I stayed up most of the night looking over those printouts," Grady said. He did look a bit worn. His razor had missed a whole section of stubble on his chin, and his eyelids were swollen. "She's got them in several accounts. There's only one problem."

"Only one?" I asked.

"I'd say about twenty-five percent of the people she took money from are dead. They were old, and she started her little home shopping network *years* ago."

"So they're dead. What does that mean?" Fanny had returned, and started rubbing the keyboard with a paper towel. "This'll burn," she explained, waving the towel.

"We want to do the right thing, don't we?" Grady asked. Bob rustled in, dropping grass in his wake. He didn't explain how he'd managed to get away from the exercise queen; didn't matter. We were all in place.

"Pick that up!" Fanny instructed, pointing to the litter on the floor.

"Of course," I said to Grady. "We want to do the right thing."

"Yes, most certainly," Ida said, nodding. "What's the right thing?"

"We give the money back. We find out how much she took from everyone and we put it back into their accounts, like we agreed before. That's the right thing."

I was getting it. "But if they're dead, we can't. And we can't give it to their kids or their grandkids, because there would be no way of explaining it. Red flags would go up everywhere."

"Exactly," Bob said, bending to pluck at the carpet. I wished he wouldn't do that.

"But what about those still living? They'll think it's pretty weird to suddenly find money added to their savings or checking or whatever," I said.

"They won't say a thing. Won't want to admit there was a reason it had disappeared in the first place," Grady said.

"So what do we do with the rest of the money?" Ida asked. "Donate it to some charity?"

We all looked at each other, and we all knew what we were thinking.

"The benevolent society of active seniors." Leave it to Fanny.

"Yoo-hoo! Mrs. List, are you home?" We all froze. It was April, come-a-calling, and by the sound of her rapid knocks, she was at my apartment door.

Grady gestured wildly for us to retreat to the computer room. We moved *en masse,* a crazed bunch of lunatics from the underworld, pressing and wrestling our way down the hall. "What do we do?" I whispered. We could still hear April rap, rap, rapping. Paco, as persistent as she, yapped while she rapped. "Mrs. List? Have you talked to Mrs. Berkowitz yet? I can't seem to raise her."

"Not unless you're Jesus," Bob said. Ida gasped at his irreverence, Fanny snickered, Grady held up his hand.

"Shhhh!" Grady said. "May. You've got to get out there and distract her. She seems determined to talk to Mrs. Berkowitz."

"She can't just walk out the door," Fanny said. "How will she explain that? Our cover will be blown for sure!"

Ida had her hands over her mouth, her eyes were growing larger by the minute, and she had that pre-swoon look going again.

"We've got to think of another way," Grady said. All eyes swung around to Bob, the king of distractions.

"Don't look at me," he said. A large frond dropped from his skirt. Anymore shedding and we'd know his religion.

"Human chain," Fanny said. She was squinting through the ends of her Coke bottles. She jutted her chin toward a window covered in aluminum foil on the south wall.

"Fu Manchu?" Ida had lost all of her color again. Her brain was beginning to shrink in upon itself by the looks of things.

"Human chain!" Fanny said. She scurried over to the window and began ripping off the aluminum foil. She had the latch undone, and the window up, before we could fully appreciate what she was doing.

April persisted in her knocking. Maybe she thought I was in the shower or taking a nap. So much for peaceful living in your waning years.

"Bob! Get your grass over here and grab my wrists!" Fanny threw her skinny legs over the window's ledge and disappeared. All I could see were her little hands hanging onto the wooden pane and an occasional feathering of white hair tossing in the breeze.

"Oh my Lord, Fanny, what are you doing?" Ida waved her hands wildly by her ears.

Bob, Grady and I raced to the window. Fanny was hanging there, legs twisting around beneath her skirt. She looked up at us and panted, "I can't hold on much longer! Ida, you're next!"

Bob grabbed Fanny's arms and hauled her back up through the window. She couldn't have weighed more than ninety pounds, which was good for Bob. He didn't look like he'd worked out much in the last few years.

"Why'd you do that?" Fanny was angry. Her human chain idea was a good one. I looked out the window then and saw we were backed up to the rear alley. Nothing down there but some old cans and a rusted shopping cart.

"There's got to be some rope or something around here." Grady headed for the hall closet."

"You want me to shimmy down a rope?" I looked around wanting a reprieve. April couldn't wait around all day. She'd leave eventually, but she was still at it, and the next door she'd be banging on was the late Mrs. Berkowitz's. No, May, you can do this. But it was two stories down, and the ground looked really hard.

"Got it." Grady came back, triumphant. He held an industrial-sized pink feather boa in his hands.

"Wait a gosh darn minute," Bob said. "I may be able to use that." Grady scowled and ignored Bob.

"Wrap this around your wrists. Hold on with your hands and we'll lower you down," Grady said.

"I don't think I can," I faltered. "I mean—it's so far." Ida was in the corner, shaking her head from side to side. The look on her face was what I imagine someone would wear after running over the family pet—in front of the kids.

"It's for the mission!" Fanny said. Her hands were balled into little fists, waist level.

"Don't think about it. Just go," Bob said. "It's what I always do."

I'll bet Bob, I'll bet.

And over I went. The ground wasn't nearly as hard as I thought it would be, but it would have been smart of me to ask Ida for one of her Depends before my free fall. The boa had held nicely for about fifteen feet, and then it snapped in half. I can still remember Bob's pained expression. He wouldn't be able to use the feathered accessory after all.

"Hurry, May!" Fanny was shooing me off. "Get around to the front now, and get rid of that nuisance."

As I was making tracks to the west side of the complex, I reminded myself—it was for the mission.

SEVENTEEN

I GOT RID OF APRIL, but it wasn't easy. She was in an absolute tizzy, asking me a dozen questions about whether or not I'd seen Mrs. Berkowitz, when, where, and what was she doing, and distraught over how she'd somehow misplaced her keys, and how some of her underwear had gone missing from the laundry room. I made up some excuse as to why my sweats were torn and greasy, and how I'd been out for a jog, and then looked at her like I was stupid. I could have explained Mrs. B. and the keys, although I didn't, but as to the underwear, Bob would probably be the best one to ask about that.

April accepted a glass of water from the tap (since my Evian was gone) and sat on my couch, dabbing at her face with a disintegrating wad of toilet paper. Hurried footsteps practically thundered on the landing so I lunged at my television. I got the volume up full blast, even covered up Paco's alarm system, and prayed April was too busy with her own worries to hear the rest of the gang making their getaway. Eventually, April finished her drink, waded through the pile of T.P. litter she'd dropped on my floor, and left. Alone in my apartment, I made phone calls all around. I didn't feel like talking in code, just told everyone to meet me at my car in twenty minutes. They were all waiting impatiently when I showed up twenty-two minutes later. I'd hosed down, put on a fresh coat of paint, and changed clothes.

"Get in," I ordered, feeling gutsy after my Airborne Ranger initiation. Bob had found a pair of shorts and a shirt somewhere, and squeezed into the back seat followed by Fanny, then Grady. Fanny looked like a little piece of meat between two buns. I threw Fanny's walker into the trunk, didn't think the air conditioner was going to be effective, so I got the top down. Ida found her place in the front, and I got behind the wheel.

I threw the Camaro into reverse, and left black marks on my way out, practically grazing Mr. Greenjeans, who popped up from behind the Dumpsters at the same time my left front tire briefly rode the sidewalk. I wanted to get to Subway before I melted. I was doing thirty when I hit the first speed bump in the Active Senior Living complex. Fanny flew up about three feet. Bob and Grady each grabbed a thigh and hauled her back in. At the second speed bump, Fanny's feet were even with Bob's shoulders, but he was ready. I jabbed the stick into third. Eat my dust, Mrs. Berkowitz.

We hit the drive-through, ordered enough sandwiches for an army, and then headed over to Starbucks. I got my usual Frappuccino, and joined the rest of the gang outside at one of the umbrella'd tables.

"Those fans aren't going to do much good after tonight. I'd say we've got until tomorrow before she starts stinking up the place," Bob said. He had mustard in the corner of his mouth. I looked around, but the lunch crowd was gone. We could talk freely.

"Grady, what's our next move?" I pulled my chair in close. My seafood and crab was heavenly, but I'd been brought up proper, so I swallowed most of it before speaking. I gave a slurp to the Frappuccino.

"We're gonna need help," Grady said. We have about five hundred envelopes to address, letters to write, and that's just the start of it."

"Letters. What for?" Bob dropped lettuce from his mouth.

"We have to tell all these people they can stop their allotments. That's how Mrs. Berkowitz has been receiving money. They set up an allotment to a fake business address, like you would to pay your phone bill or your Internet bill. It doesn't look fishy to the banks that way. Mrs. Berkowitz has her phony business, she gets paid by all of these people, and her bank doesn't get suspicious."

"So they stop the allotments themselves?" Ida said.

"They can, but even if they don't, that's okay, because we're setting up our own little business," Grady continued. We all leaned in. This was getting interesting. "We have to go to a bank, set up a corporation and transfer all of Mrs. Berkowitz's money into the new account."

"Hold on. First of all, I don't think just anybody can walk up and ask the bank to take money out of one account and put it into another. What if her son's name is on her account?" I asked.

"Slow down," Grady said. "I've thought of all that. First of all, I looked through everything. Her son's name isn't on any of her stuff. He's been really slick about it. I think he figures if Mrs. Berkowitz were ever caught, what would they do to an eighty-five-year-old lady? She'd take a slap on the wrist, and a little community service. But if he were tied in, it would mean hard time. He trusted her enough, apparently, to give him a part of the action in cash, or personal checks. Something like that."

"We write the letters. How are you going to make the transfers?" Ida asked.

"That's where you come in, May," Grady was looking at me. They were all looking at me. I choked and coughed. Not another mission.

"Remember when I said you were about her size? You have to *become* Mrs. Berkowitz." I choked again. Ida thumped my back.

"As far as I can tell, Mrs. Berkowitz only goes out of her apartment twice a month. Once on the first, and once on the fifteenth. Her son probably comes to pick her up. That's when they go to the bank. There's a lot of activity on her accounts at that time. It's payday for most people on those days, and that's when banks are busy. Less chance for people to notice them coming and going. She's got a safety deposit box too that we'll have to get into."

"I never see him." Bob was still chewing. "I never see her son. I don't hear him, I don't see him. When could he come pick her up?"

"Maybe she meets him. I don't know. But I think it would be a good idea for all of you to remember what today is."

"The last day of the month." I choked. Ida began thumping again.

EIGHTEEN

AND SO THERE I WAS, and you can see what I mean when I say I may have lost my mind somewhere in the midst of all the confusion. It's not so hard to believe, when you consider all I'd been through in those few days. Extortion, bald-headed cuckoo birds, golfing cripples, cross-dressing firemen, horny grandpas, special agent grandmas, and frustrated soldiers of fortune. The fact that someone may have wanted me dead paled in the light of all that was happening around me. I barely even had time to think about that little issue. That is, until the phone call.

The gang sat at Starbucks under the little green umbrella, sweltering and tossing ideas around, when I heard a muffled ringing. Grady grabbed at his ears and began playing with his hearing aids, I stopped slurping at the last bit of slush from the bottom of my cup, Ida and Bob looked perplexed, but Fanny dug into the bottom of her walker bag and lifted a singing cell phone.

"Only use it in emergencies. This must be our contact," Fanny said. She looked both ways, then hunkered down in her chair and pushed the button on her phone. She shielded the receiver with her free hand. "Fanny here, whatcha got?" It must be the guy from the forensics lab. The call I'd been waiting for, and I felt my pulse gather speed. My emotions were similar to those I experienced when sitting in the doctor's office, waiting to hear if I really did have a tumor or the big C or polyps. A negative would be a relief, but a positive would mean a little extra attention, and affirmation that I wasn't a hypochondriac, that I didn't have Munchausens, and I wasn't making more of my aches and pains than an old lady should. I was boring holes into Fanny, but she kept turning away from me, and I couldn't read her at all.

"I'm going to get another drink," I said abruptly. Everyone around the table looked a bit stunned, wondering how I could leave when the big news was on the horizon. If it was bad news it could wait. Besides, my heart was doing a tap dance in my chest, and to sit still was more than I could manage. I got a monster sized Frappuccino and sucked at it hurriedly before returning for the *big news*. I wanted to get a super brain freeze going, just to numb up. It didn't make any difference; I knew when I walked to the table that it wasn't good.

"Enough rat poison to noose a moose," Fanny said. She almost seemed delighted to announce this. "That is, if the amounts in the crumbs were indicative of what was in the rest of the load."

"It can't be," I said. The dull pounding in my head

was way more than what a frozen drink could manu-
facture, in fact, the numbness in my brain had reached
all the way to my toes. I looked around the table at the
sympathetic faces, waiting for Ida to say, "There, there,
it's not so bad," or for Grady to wink and lift a thumb,
or for Bob to say "What? What?" but they just
squirmed. Bob sawed his straw up and down through
his plastic coffee cup lid and it made a rude honking
sound, Grady cleared his throat, and Ida's lips were
pressed together so tightly they'd lost all form. It was
Fanny who broke the silence.

"You know," she said, hunkering down even further
in her chair, "there may be a bead on the mark right now."
Fanny shielded her eyes and scanned the building roofs
across the street. "Could be someone in that window up
there with a scope and a full magazine even as we speak."

It was impossible not to peer out from under the
umbrella, although since I was *the mark* I just grabbed
a quick look, and then fell back into the shadows.

"No, no, come to think of it," Fanny said. "That
wouldn't be the perp's M.O. Too messy."

Ida started fanning herself furiously with her dainty
napkin. "I'm sure it was just an accident May, some
horrible oversight," she said. "I'm sure nobody's trying
to kill you at all." The napkin picked up speed. "Maybe
they were really trying to kill Mrs. Berkowitz after all.
I mean, wouldn't they have tried again by now? And
besides, who would want to kill you?" Ida was beginning to wheeze.

"Slow down now, Ida." Grady picked up his napkin and joined the fan fair.

"It could have been just a silly mistake!" Ida was turning blue around her white lips. "A really tragic mistake, but a, ah, ah—"

I had never seen anyone roll their eyes into their head before. You hear people say it, but there was Ida, rolling away. When I was a little girl, I once I had a doll whose eyes unplugged from their sockets and got lost, rattling around in her empty plastic head, but that didn't really count. Grady got a pitcher of ice water and had Ida coming around before she slithered to the pavement. Poor Ida, she really wasn't handling this well. "It's the heat and all the excitement," I consoled. "Look here. You haven't even touched your lunch." I patted Ida's wrists. "Let's get you back to your apartment."

I took the speed bumps a little more carefully on our return. Ida had her head on the back of the car seat, eyes closed, coming around only when I popped the trunk to retrieve Fanny's walker. Grady helped her to the apartment. There wasn't much time to play nursemaid—we had work to do.

"We've got to hurry." Grady handed out assignments, tasks written neatly on yellow legal paper. He'd been busy last night. Ida may have had one gasket left after blowing the one at Starbucks, but I didn't know how helpful she would be. We were in her apartment, collecting our wits and perusing our duties, gearing up for the *mission*. Fanny had swung by her apartment to get supplies, and was standing, partially hidden by the curtains, with binoculars pressed against her glasses.

"Mr. Greenjeans is talking to April by the laundry room," she reported. "And, oh yes, here come Mr. and Mrs. Ramirez. Wait a minute, wait a minute! No, nothing in the basket except laundry." Fanny sucked in her breath and swung around, plastering her back against the wall. Her binoculars swung from her neck. "I think they saw me."

"Come on Fanny," Bob growled. "We need your help."

Fanny pouted and grabbed the yellow sheet held in Bob's hand. "What about her?" She was tilting her head in Ida's direction. The poor woman had molded herself into her rocking chair the minute we entered the room, and hadn't moved since. Could have been that was the last gasket after all.

"I'll make her a sandwich," I whispered. Didn't really matter though, Ida wasn't seeing or hearing much of anything. If she didn't move soon, someone would be scooping out her Depends. I listened as Grady explained our next move. I found bread and some cheese and slapped mayo on, squished the pieces together and looked for a plate.

"We have to go today. Banks close at four so that gives us about two hours," he said. I opened the cabinets, found glasses, cups, opened the next cupboard and dropped the sandwich on the floor.

"May, you should be listening to this." Fanny

shuffled over to the small kitchenette. She dropped her binoculars in the sink.

"You two okay?" Grady sauntered over to Fanny and said "Holy Mother."

"What is going on in…?" Bob stepped up behind Grady and said, "Whoooooah."

Together we all turned slowly and looked at Ida.

"A terrible mistake!" She started rocking hard. "It was the baking soda! Look at the box, it looks just like the box of Rid Rat!" Her eyes were going again.

I reached for the plate in the cupboard, the one with tiny blue flowers around the edges, the one with a gold stripe along the outside of the flowers, a plate identical to the one that had found its way onto my porch, into Mrs. Berkowitz's apartment, and now on its way to the city landfill.

"You tried to kill May? What did she ever do to you? Citizen's arrest I say, citizen's arrest!" Fanny looked as if she were about to tackle Ida and cuff her. I was pretty certain she had a pair of iron bracelets in that little walker bag of hers.

"Hold on." Bob held out his hands and struggled for control. He produced a box from under the sink with the words Rid Rat on the front. If it weren't for the skull and crossbones, I suppose one could confuse it for the baking soda he pulled from the pantry. Close to the same size and color. It could happen.

"I didn't mean it May, I really didn't!" Ida started blubbering good. Pistons, gaskets, the whole darn transmission gone. "I was just trying to make you feel welcome, and then you took my brownies over to Mrs. Berkowitz and then…I saw the box, and then…"

Fanny said something like "Hmmph!" and pulled off her bifocals. "You need these more than I do." She tossed them toward Ida, who recoiled as if they would bite her. Ida rocked harder until her feet started flying off the floor: back down, then up again.

"I just wanted to be a good neighbor!" Ida said in hitching spasms.

Bob startled us all when he began to bray. He stood in the kitchen, holding the boxes and laughed so hard his belly took on a rhythm of its own. "It's perfect, don't you see?" He set the boxes down to rub his watering eyes. "Divine intervention! No other way to explain it. We had a rat in the complex, and Ida got rid of it for us. Absolutely perfect. I don't think I'll ever look at a brownie the same way again." His belly was bouncing again.

"I don't think it's very funny, Bob." Fanny frowned at him. "That could have been May Bell here. Did you think of that? And now that we know Ida is a murderess, what are we gonna do about that, hmm?"

Ida groaned loudly.

"But she's not," Grady said softly, moving to stand behind Ida. He pressed gently on her shoulders, calming the rocking. "It was a mistake. Nothing more, a rather convenient mistake, but she didn't mean to do any harm."

I glanced toward the balcony, caught Grady's eye

and knew he was thinking what I was thinking. There were at least two dozen little cookies out there, and now I'm sure, more than one dead mouse. Dieting does have more than a few benefits.

I could see Grady had a calming effect on Ida; she wasn't trying to propel herself across the living room via the rocker anymore, and she had actually smiled a little at his reassurance.

"They can trace these things you know. They'll find rat poison in Mrs. Berkowitz and it'll be an all-out investigation. They'll get search warrants, lie detectors, latents. I think we'd better get Ida out of town." Fanny found her glasses and settled them back on her nose.

"We'll worry about that later. Mrs. Berkowitz isn't going anywhere for the time being, and we've got a meeting at the bank." Grady turned to me, in charge. "First we've got to get you into some different clothes. May? You ready?"

Me ready? Grady looked at me expectantly with his thumbs at half-mast. When I gave my reluctant assent, he thrust his thumbs in the air jubilantly and proclaimed, "Let's go then!"

WE LEFT IDA AND FANNY to their own lists of tasks. They were to begin the arduous job of addressing envelopes and stuffing form letters into them. Grady had printed out a heavy stack of "You are no longer obligated to continue your allotment to the Save the Cats Foundation" forms, and it was going to take the two women the rest of the afternoon to get them folded and inserted. I saw Fanny extract two pairs of yellow surgical gloves from her walker bag and hand a pair to Ida, explaining too, that they shouldn't lick the envelopes, but use sponges. "Can't take the chance of spittle DNA." She explained. One of these days I would have to get a look in that bag.

As I trailed along behind Grady, I could hear the voice of my husband as if he were walking along beside me. "*'Tweren't nothing May Bell, just a harmless little steff meeting with Staffy, I mean, a staff meeting with Steffy. All of the offices were being renovated and it was just logical to hold our conference in the supply closet.* I had to wonder if she'd been taking *dicktation* while I rubbed calluses on my knees mopping up all the little curly hairs on our bathroom floor.

I went back to the pivotal moment in our relationship when I heard him singing that song on the phone: "I'm just a luv mucheen and I won't work for nobody but you…" Who had been on the other end of the line? Did he have cute little ditties for each of his conquests? I wished he could see me now in my new take-charge strut, picking up the pace, passing Grady, giving him my own confident thumbs-up, sticking out my tongue at Paco, before I tackled the stairs to Mrs. Berkowitz's place, wondering what he would think of me now. No more curly hair bathroom duty for this girl.

NINETEEN

"WE'RE RUNNING OUT of time." Grady shut the door behind me. His dark eyebrows were shaking hands in the middle of his creased forehead. He had to talk loudly over the fans, and we were both trying to avoid taking a peek at what was beginning to stink up the place on the couch. "I'll find her purse, you get busy in the closet. We'll need all of her I.D. and her safety deposit box key."

"What if you can't find it?" I couldn't help myself. I peeked at the couch.

"You just worry about getting into costume. I'll do the rest. If I can't find it we'll just forget it. Her son can have what's in there for all I care…"

"But what if there's evidence? You know, papers, documents, stuff he can use?"

"Right. I'm not thinking. I'll get it. You go get yourself ready." Grady peeked at the couch. Our eyes met.

"She's sinking," I said, understanding what it must have felt like to be the captain of the Titanic. "She's smaller, I think."

Grady peeked again. "But she's smiling."

I never could keep myself from staring at a good car

accident. I took an appraising look. The couch seemed to be swallowing Mrs. Berkowitz whole. She looked a little flat, her face had pulled down and those big, yellow teeth of hers were saying, "Cheese."

When I came out of the bathroom I *was* Mrs. Berkowitz. I'd made use of her most memorable frocks and locks. There I stood, red braided wig, stiletto heels and pleated white skirt. I wore an orange cowl-necked sweater and fishnet hose. If nothing else, the ensemble would detract from my face, but just to make sure, I'd covered my face with enough of her makeup to make even a careful observer confused. I had the smell of Oil of Olay, although I was thinking at this stage it might have been best to call it Oil of Olé! The plan was coming together, we were standing before the bull, and I was never more nervous in my life.

"I had to rummage around in her pockets for this." Grady held up a dainty eel-skinned wallet, and pulled out her driver's license. "Don't know why she had this, she never drove anywhere."

"It was on her?" I shuddered.

"You're passable." Grady looked at me then at the picture. "She was even a bit heavier back then, which makes you almost perfect."

"Thanks a lot."

"Okay. You're perfect." Grady backpedaled and for that I was grateful, if not begrudging. "You pull this off and I owe you dinner and a movie."

Good ol' Grade. I winked at him and rustled my skirt. "I'll take you up on that. Just leave your Viagra at home."

"Spoil sport."

What in the heck was I doing? I reminded myself I'd been brought up proper and cut the flirts. Wasn't quite right with a woman decomposing on the couch.

We stood, wondering how we could make our way to my car, when a scream sent Grady racing to the balcony door. I looked for a place to hide.

Grady chuckled and let the blinds fall. "That's our cue," he said.

There was no problem getting to my car. All able bodied residents—and some not so able bodied—of the Active Senior Center were shuffling, limping and rolling toward the swimming pool with Mr. Greenjeans leading the pack. More screams distracted me, but Grady grabbed my hand and pulled me toward the stairwell.

"It's just Bob," he explained. "He's clearing the way."

"Sounded like April," I said.

"A screaming fleet afoot," Grady agreed.

I gave Mrs. Berkowitz a smart salute and raced after Grady. As I thumped over the speed bumps, I wondered what Bob had dreamed up this time.

"There it is," I said. The bank looked like a crouching, brick tiger, and I was about to walk through its yawning mouth. Grady was leaning forward, drumming his hands on the dash as we waited for the light to change.

"There it is," he echoed.

"How do I look?" I checked the mirror.

"Ridiculous."

I leaned my head back and howled like a banshee. Grady cracked his knees under the dash and I smiled. "Just practicing," I said.

"Did you have to do that, May?" Grady rubbed his knees.

"That's Mrs. Berkowitz to you. Just getting in character my friend."

"I don't remember her screaming like that."

"How's this?" I laughed like a witch.

"That, I remember."

"Gives you the creeps, doesn't it?" I smiled again then leaned close to Grady's face. "Why didn't you kick him out?" I said in a low growl.

"What?" Grady was looking scared.

"Oh never mind. I'm just a little punchy. It happens when I'm nervous."

"We've sat through two lights now, do you think you can park this thing?" Grady looked at his watch. I twisted the wheel and found a place in the lot across the street. No surveillance cameras and that was good.

I knew the drill; Grady had hammered the details into my brain on the way to the bank. It sounded simple. Announce that I was retiring from my "business" and that I would need to withdraw all of my money and close all accounts. Mrs. Berkowitz was moving to the Caymans to live out the rest of her life in luxury.

"What about the safety deposit box?" I stopped on the sidewalk and turned to Grady.

"Never fear, my dear." Grady reached into his pocket and brought out a tarnished gold key. "Found it in the aquarium. The little scuba diver had more than jewels in that treasure chest. Like some other men I know, ahem."

"I don't believe it! How did you think to look in there?" I closed my hand over his and took the key.

"Brains." Grady tapped his forehead. "Not really. She had a note in some of her computer stuff; didn't leave much to chance or a faulty memory."

"Good thing for us. I just hope you didn't overlook anything." We were in front of the bank now and I could feel those fingers in my stomach fluttering around again.

"You okay?" Grady asked. He probably noticed my makeup was slipping a little around the jaw line.

"I've never done anything like this before."

"I'm happy to hear that. But if it will make you feel any better, I have. What you want to do is keep the teller off balance. I'll set the stage; you just go in and give the best-darned performance of your life. There are a lot of old fogies depending on it."

"That's it Grade, pile on the pressure."

"I do what I can," Grady said. If I knew how, I'd have given him a scissor, but good.

We went in. The lobby of the bank had emptied out most of its customers. I got the feeling that the employees were eager to get home. There was only one teller working the windows, requiring Grady to fall in line behind a couple with a crying baby. The girl looked about seventeen, and she was bouncing the baby on a hip. The smell of used Pampers fluffed out with each bounce. I got behind Grady and hunched my shoulders, both to set a vision, and to use his wide back as an odor shield. Grady didn't seem to notice. He was fiddling with his hearing aids. He popped out one, then the other, and palmed them.

"What are you doing?" I hissed.

"Shhhh!" Grady said without turning. The girl spun around and glared at Grady. "Shhhh, there now, little one." Grady grabbed a fat little finger and the baby hiccupped and stopped crying for a minute. The mom looked at her hand in Grady's and jerked it away. "Sorry miss. Thought I was holding the little one's toes."

"Next!" The teller got busy with the couple. I poked Grady in the back.

"Look at us," Grady said, out of the corner of his mouth. "A couple old farts, a little on the diminished capacity side. Use whatcha got, May Bell, work it, baby, work it."

"Don't forget the cameras," I said, wanting Grady to feel the same panic I was swimming in. When I say swimming, it wasn't too far from the truth. If I dribbled any more under my arms I'd need water wings just to stay afloat. I pinned my elbows in close to hide the circles.

"Next!" It was Grady's turn then, and I was alone.

That's when my legs began to jiggle. My thighs were flapping together so loudly I took a wider stance to give them room. My size seven feet were sliding around in Mrs. Berkowitz's size eight shoes and the stiletto heels were about as stable as ballpoint pens on the marble floor. All the shaking and flapping and stance-widening put me off balance. I worked hard to correct, scooting my feet back together in a toe-heel, toe-heel motion, knees going in then out, in then out, and to those watching, I'm sure they expected me to bend right over and do a Bob dance with my hands in front of my knees, criss-crossing back and forth. Cha, cha, cha.

"Ma'am? Are you alright?" Her name was Misty. I read it on the placard by her teller window. Misty was weaving around trying to see past Grady, who did his best to match her, weave for weave. I was gulping air. Misty was about to come over the counter. Grady put up a reassuring hand. "I'll see what I can do."

"What's going on, May?" Grady was talking, although his lips didn't move. He just smiled calmly and took my elbow. A kindly old man consoling a feeble old woman. I grabbed his jacket and pulled his face close to mine.

"I can't do this!" I whispered loudly.

"Misty," Grady said politely over his shoulder. "I think this lady needs a chair."

"Of course," Misty said, her face showing deep concern. She picked up the phone, and soon a gentleman rushed over with a desk chair on wheels. He pushed it behind my calves and the stiletto heels scooted out, depositing my bottom.

"There you go, Mrs. Berkowitz," the man said. I shot a look at Grady. "I'll just have Mr. Hansom take care of you at his desk. It's okay now. I see you're wearing the red today? My favorite." The man steered me over to a large walnut desk behind a glass partition. "He's new, but he'll take good care of you."

"I'm sure he will," Grady patted my hand. "I think I'll just stay with this dear lady if you don't mind, just in case she needs anything."

Thanks, Grade. Thanks a bunch.

We were alone, waiting for Mr. Hansom. The Plexiglas cubicle offered a bit of privacy.

"That guy thought I was Mrs. Berkowitz!" I said. I grabbed a tissue off of the walnut desk and dabbed at my melting neck.

"You sound surprised." Grady plucked more tissues and held them out for me.

"I just didn't think, well, I just don't know what to think."

"It's working perfectly. Look at the clock. We're all alone now, it's right at closing time, and this guy will be in a hurry to get us out of his hair. Besides, he's new, so calm down. He'd believe you if you tell him you're Mrs. Netanyahu."

"You sound pretty sure of yourself. By the way, what were you doing up there with Misty?"

"I was just trying to get her a bit flustered. Told her

I needed a loan for food. When she tried to ask me a few questions I put these near her mouth and asked her to speak into them." Grady held out his hearing aids nestled in his palm. "Didn't matter though, you took care of things for me. What was that jig you were doing out there?"

"Shut up, Grady, I could have had a heart attack. I wasn't trained for this type of work."

"Looked kinda cute, really."

"Don't start with me, or I swear, I'll take my keys and leave you here to take the next bus home. Now stick those things back in your ears. Somebody's coming."

TWENTY

"Nurse! Get that gurney over here. We've got a dozen interns coming through in a few minutes, and we need to teach them the proper procedures for connecting EKG leads."

"Right away Dr. List, would you like to use Mr. Franks for your demonstration?"

"That guy? No thanks. You'll do just fine. I think it would be in our best interest though to practice a few times just to get it right. Hop right up here."

"This gurney is pretty small, doctor; wouldn't it be better to use one of the beds?"

"Good thinking, Nurse Bambie! Now just crawl right up and help me get these leads properly placed."

"But doctor, I'd have to open my shirtfront for that!"

"Exactly, Nurse Bambie, all in the name of science, all for advanced medicine; now don't be shy, let the buttons fall where they may!"

"Whatever you say Dr. List; I'll have to get rid of my bra too, it's in the way."

"Hope it's one of those front connector kinds, we're closing in on zero hour."

"Well as a matter of fact I think it is...ooops! Would you look at that? I forgot to wear a bra today."

"Glory be! Nurse Bambie, you really are on top of things."

"Thank you doctor! That's what I always hear about you!"

"Why, thank you nurse, and just so you know how much I appreciate your attitude, I think I'll put you in for a big promotion!"

I had to do something just to get my wits about me, but my mental wanderings almost blinded me to Grady's frantic gesticulations.

"It's him!" Grady was saying, and having a good old-fashioned conniption.

"Who?" I was back in the moment.

"HIM! It's Mrs. Berkowitz's son! Oh man, oh man, oh man, Mr. Hansom is *Mrs. Berkowitz's son,* and he's coming this way!"

"Her son?" I swiveled in my chair to get a look but Grady held me still.

"We've got to get out of here. Oh man. This isn't working at all like I planned."

"Think, Grady! What are we going to do?"

"I don't know! I just don't know! Wait. He's talking

to someone right now. Let's just get up right now and leave as quickly as we can."

I stood up and wobbled. I could see a rather thin, small man, not bad looking, respectable enough in a blue pin stripe, discussing something on a yellow legal pad with the guy who'd recognized me as Mrs. Berkowitz. This was bad.

"Do you think that guy will say something to him?"

"Don't care, doesn't matter, we've just got to get going. Just walk, May, scoot!"

And then he saw us.

The look on his face was priceless. I must have looked like the proverbial deer in the headlights; he looked like a man who had just seen his identical twin for the first time. Our mouths were both open and hanging.

I'd seen women running on tiny spike heels in movies, and I always poo-pooed the notion that anyone could move with any amount of speed or agility on those things, but it's possible. I'm here to tell you it's possible. It's even more possible if a man has his arm around your waist lifting you along every third or fourth step. By the time I hit the R on my floor shifter, every ounce of air had been squeezed from my lungs and my fishnet crotch was around my lower thighs, but I worked that clutch like Mario Andretti.

We had to get back to the Senior Center. We'd been fingered, and it was time for our backup plan.

"We do have a backup plan, don't we, Grade?" My

chin was trembling hard. I wanted a nap, a shower, and a Butterfinger.

"It's gonna be tricky, but we don't have any other choice. Don't go home yet. We've got to make a stop."

CompUSA came into view about the time my chin stopped trembling, but then my hands took over the spasmodic dance. "What if he's not working tonight?" I grabbed the keys and hobbled along behind Grady's long strides.

"We'll get his phone number. We'll get his address. We'll hold the whole darn place hostage until we find him."

"Right. Right," I said.

We paced the aisles gathering stares along the way. By this time, my face must have looked like a runny oil painting. I hitched at my fishnets.

"Can I help you?" The bored, impatient voice was unmistakable. Grady and I breathed collective sighs.

"Lance, I mean Brad. I'm so happy you're here." Lance-Brad leaned his head to the side and cocked his eyebrow. A new lance accompanied the first skewer. Or maybe it was a brad. Either way it looked painful.

"Having trouble getting your windows open again?" Brad's lips pushed out a tiny snicker.

"Having trouble finding your real hair color?" Grady jabbed. I pinched him and he shut up.

Brad didn't take offense, probably had practice in absolution, or just operated on simple "ignore."

"How are you feeling?" I looked both ways, then back at Brad-Lance.

"How should I be feeling?" Brad looked both ways.

"I think you're feeling bad. Really bad. Case of the worst diarrhea a person ever had." I glanced around again.

"How bad is this case of the Hershey squirts?" Brad-Lance closed the distance between us.

"Five hundred dollars bad," I said. Grady made a throaty noise, so I elbowed him in the ribs.

"Come to think of it, I probably shouldn't have had that burger from the In and Out."

"Exactly."

"Faster out, than in." Brad-Lance loosened his tie and cockeyed his name tag. "Headquarters then?"

"Ten minutes," I said.

"Nice ensemble," Brad-Lance said. "My girlfriend would like those shoes."

I reached down, grabbed the pumps and shoved them into his hand.

"Consider it a down payment."

"WELL IT'S ABOUT TIME!" Fanny met us at the door. "The bank closed over an hour ago. Where have you two been?"

Mrs. Gateway rushed over to take me in her embrace, and then she hugged Grady and stood back, wringing her hands. "We were so worried! We thought something awful had happened!"

"Something awful did happen," I said, and

motioned for Grady to turn around so I could squirm out of the sliding fishnets.

"You've lost your shoes!" Ida said. She started chewing her knuckles.

"And my mind," I added.

"What happened? Did you get the money transferred?" Fanny thrust her chin out awaiting the verdict.

"No. No we didn't." Grady looked defeated. I felt guilty, but I'm not sure exactly why. Maybe if I hadn't done my cha, cha, cha, we'd have been in the clear by now. Ida's table was covered with fat, little, white envelopes. The girls had been busy. I didn't see Bob anywhere.

"My hand's cramped on me at least fifteen times, and I'm swallowing bile all this time that you're out, and you come back to say the operation's been struck. So what's up?" Fanny lifted her chin a little higher and poked it at us like a dagger.

"Her son works in the bank. Grady recognized him. They call him Mr. Hansom, I was having an anxiety attack or something, and we couldn't use the window, and then Misty made some guy get a chair and I was pushed over to this little place, and we saw him, and we had to run." I got it out in a rush.

Fanny listened, then looked at Grady.

"Now you. What happened?" I pulled off the wig and scratched at my scalp. What if Mrs. Berkowitz had cooties? Oooeee. Hadn't thought of that.

Grady explained with more clarity and calm. Then, after a long pause he said, "I've been thinking about it. They said Mrs. Berkowitz's son is new at the bank. As far as I can figure he's getting her account ready for a big transfer. She changes banks about every two years or so. It wouldn't be a far cry for him to go in, establish himself in the bank, make some transfers and changes, while probably padding the kitty, and then ducking out. It doesn't draw a lot of suspicion that way, and he uses an alias. All this time, I thought he'd been taking his mom to the bank. If he was, he didn't show his face."

"I thought he was a P.I.," Fanny accused.

"Was a P.I., was," Grady corrected.

Fanny smacked her fist into her hand. "He's a slick one that guy. Probably casing the joint all this time." Her wide eyes got wider. "So he's gonna put two and two together. How're we gonna off the perp?"

Ida blanched.

"We're not gonna *off* the perp. We're gonna outwit him."

"And how do you plan to do that, Mr. 'I had to abort the mission'?" Fanny widened her already wide eyes.

There was a knock at the door. Ida grabbed a table-cloth and threw it over the envelopes. She shoved a bowl of fruit on top of the mound. Cool, Ida, looks real natural.

"Here's how," Grady said calmly. He opened the door and presented Brad-Lance.

"Anybody here got a bottle of Imodium?" Brad was beaming. I couldn't help myself. I gave him a tight squeeze.

We crowded around Grady's computer, waiting for Lance to work his magic. He knelt on the floor, fiddling with something that looked like a briefcase.

"Can't work with that dinosaur if we're gonna do what you say." Lance said, then looked at Grady. "Sorry Pops. Just the way it is."

"That's Mr. Pops to you. I mean—oh, never mind. Can you do it?"

Lance-Brad lifted a tiny computer thing, which I later learned was a laptop. Go figure. He was plugging in wires and pushing buttons. "If I can't do it..." he started.

"It can't be done," we all chorused.

"Right."

"Oh May Bell, this is all so exciting and so dangerous!" Ida was clutching her bosom.

"Let me get this straight," Fanny was saying. "You're whacking in?"

"Hacking. Hacking in. To the bank's computer system. We'll make all of the transfers by computer. It's done all the time, only you usually have to have some kind of password."

"It's impossible. Can't be done." Fanny glowered at me. I knew I'd really blown it and I wanted to wither.

"There is a way." Lance waved his hands at us, a signal we were to leave him at it.

"Well if there is a way, and you could do it before, why haven't you?" Fanny asked.

Lance looked at her under heavy lids. "Who says I haven't?"

Ida gasped.

"Let him work now, girls." Grady herded us back up to Ida's apartment where we got busy filling envelopes. There must have been hundreds.

"How much money are we talking, Grady?" Fanny dipped a sponge in a bowl of water and hammered down an envelope flap.

"Don't bang it, Fanny, just smooth it," Ida said.

"You do it your way, I'll do it mine." Fanny banged another one.

"Millions," Grady said quietly. He was glancing out the window. We all stopped working.

"Did you say millions?" Ida asked.

"Millions. She's been at it a long time."

"All those people. Tsk, tsk. What a shame." Ida smoothed.

"Well the buck stops here. One way or another, it stops here."

"I'm worried, Grady." I almost didn't want to say it, but it had to be said. "Tomorrow her son will be here to pick her up for her trip to the bank. He'll find her dead, her will more than likely names him as the sole beneficiary, and he'll have access to her accounts. Everything. We won't have a chance at that money after today."

"I was thinking of that. Maybe we should offer Brad more money."

"Maybe we should."

After that, we were all quiet, stuffing, smoothing or banging, shoving envelopes into a cardboard box.

Finally, as the sun fell behind the mountains, we were finished, and exhausted. Still, there was no word from Brad. I needed a change of clothes. Ida gave me a long sweater to throw over my Berkowitz duds, and I forged the labyrinth back to my apartment.

Nothing had changed in my little milk-carton abode; it smelled sour, felt sour and was still hot, but I had my things around me, and a shower woke me up and gave me new energy. I looked at the litter of Mrs. Berkowitz clothes on the bathroom floor, stained with my makeup. Her wig hung over the doorknob. I knew I had to get them back into her apartment, but didn't have the desire to do it just yet. I wandered over to my new computer and remembered her saying, *He really set me up!* He sure did, Mrs. B. He sure did. I wondered how I would feel the first time I used the keyboard, re-membering the old woman leaning over me with her leaky blue eyes asking why I hadn't kicked *him* out. Maybe that would be my first story. "Why I Didn't Kick Him Out," by M. B. List.

The zipper on my pants slid up with ease. I stepped on the scales, just because, and saw the needle stop much too soon. Another three pounds. That's what stress in the gangland will do to a gal. I heard some voices outside, Paco started to bark, and the Mariachi music wailed out. Good old mariachis. Green Cards or no, they were okay in my book. Another little thing I'd learned from Mrs. Berkowitz's *data*.

I got the clothes in a brown paper bag and shoved

them under my bed for the time being. My phone hadn't rung, so I was pretty sure I had time before heading back to Ida's. I wondered about Bob, and I wondered a little bit about Ted.

"Looks like you've really done it May Bell, you can stand on your own two bunions. Who'da thunk it, my little Maybe Baby? Who'da thunk it?"

Shut up, Ted. Go boink an intern.

WHEN I GOT BACK to Ida's, there was a palpable excitement in the air.

"He's done it May! He's done it! Come on, see for yourself!" Ida grabbed my hand and we bustled into Grady's apartment.

"You earned this one, Brad." Grady had a Heine in his hand, and shoved one in mine, after giving one to the pimply nerd beside him.

"Mission accomplished."

Fanny was sitting cross-legged in a chair. "Never doubted it for a minute," she said, and sucked on her green bottle. She burped loudly and didn't apologize.

"What is it?" I caught the excitement and looked at everyone.

"Let's just say, Mr. Hansom is one broke dude," Brad said. Grady pumped his hand and clinked bottles with the boy. Best friends.

"How did you do it?" I insisted.

"Sometimes, it's just best not to know these things," Grady said. He and Brad exchanged winks.

Brad was a sharp cookie. The look on his face said Grady had given him the short, and dare I say, sweet version of why it had become necessary to include him in all of this underworld business. He actually looked quite proud to be of some help.

"The less you know, the less you can tell if they torture you or if they give you some of that sodium pentathlon," Fanny said. She burped again, a full open mouth belch. No apology.

"Okay, I give. Now what?" I wasn't about to believe it could be that easy.

"It's going to take me a while to go through all the records and return the money to those still alive, but as long as the money is where her son can't get at it, I have time for that. Actually, I'm looking forward to it. Feel sort of like a Shriner."

"Drink up then, Shriners!" Brad said, and tipped his bottle.

"To the Shriners!" Ida bellowed, and tossed back.

"If there's nothing else, I guess I'll be going now," Brad said. He tucked a wad of bills in his jeans pocket and handed Grady his beer. "Better let this go. Got finals tomorrow."

"Finals?"

"Yeah. Working on my MBA. Mom told me I had a head for business."

There were exuberant hugs all around, which lit up

Brad's acne like fire, but he didn't resist. I was going to miss that boy.

"Where is Bob?" I asked when Brad was gone.

"Yeah," Fanny said. "Where is Bob?" I haven't seen him since he locked himself in the laundry room with April Fleet. Never saw such a crowd."

"He did what?" I laughed loudly. I was feeling fine.

"Oh yeah. You didn't hear? I thought April was going to strangle him until Mr. Greenjeans stepped in. Mr. Scissorhands had Bob in a headlock, and was gouging away. April was just standing there screaming. What a show."

I shook my head. "I hope he's okay."

"Of course he's okay," said a familiar voice from the front door.

Ida squealed and started clapping her hands. "Bob!" we all cried, and rushed him.

"Whoa, gotta beer for the one who sacrificed his body, pride and everything else for the cause?"

Grady handed him a beer. "Should've remembered to lock that door. Get in here, son, and give us the scoop."

I DON'T KNOW IF it was the beer or the effects of constant tension that did us in, but by the time Bob finished his story we were all howling like hyenas.

As he told it, Bob caught April Fleet at the door of Mrs. Berkowitz, yoo-hooing and rapping away. He'd gone back to remove the fans, but only got as far as the bottom of the stairs when he noticed April's purple hulk. He had to act fast.

"What? What?" he cried, stopping her hand in mid-rap. Then he started the show. He'd been in shorts and a shirt as you remember, quite modest for old Bob, so when he pulled his shirt over his head with bumps and grinds, April simply averted her eyes and kept calling out. "Mrs. Berkowitz, it's the apartment manager. Can I have a word? Mrs. Berkowitz!"

Bob grew more anxious. He needed a new deal.

"I seen her!" Bob called out, and this got April's attention because she'd never heard him say anything more than "What? What?"

"Where is she, Bob?" April dashed down to take Bob by the shoulders. She shook him so hard his teeth rattled. "I can't get her to answer her door."

"Your underwear?" Bob paused for dramatic effect. "She's been taking them. She's down there right now hauling them out of the dryer."

April went white, then red. Another minute and Bob thought she'd go for the full old glory.

"Come on," April demanded. "Show me."

"I followed her down the sidewalk, her backside was just a swinging," Bob said. "I've never seen April so mad. She was leaning forward like she was charging a hill. I still didn't know what I was going to do once we got to the laundry room. I knew this one had to be good, or she'd be right back at Mrs. Berkowitz's door, and the way she had her mouth set I didn't doubt for one minute that she'd use a crowbar to get that door open."

"Was Mrs. Berkowitz really stealing her underwear?" Ida asked, worried. "That's pretty sick." We all looked at her. "Well it is," she said primly.

I caught Fanny out of the corner of my eye. She had her hand up, ready to smack Ida in the back of the head. I shot her a "better not" look, and she pouted, but let it go.

"So when we got to the laundry room we were alone, all the dryers were done and the only thing going was a wash load on spin. That's when I got this idea. I grabbed April under the armpits and threw her up on the washer. Not easy, I might add, think I got a hernia. I'd heard some women find it a turn-on to be sitting on a rumbling washer and I told her so."

Ida and Grady shot each other fast glances. Ida turned red. So, I thought, I guess the old laundry room is good for more than just whiter whites and vibrant colors.

"And that's when she started screaming," Fanny said. She pulled her glasses off and fogged them with hot breath. She put them on without rubbing them with her shirttail like I expected. Now her world was in soft focus. Sort of like my brain these days.

"No! That's what's so great!" Bob lifted his bottle and drained it. The rest of us stood there, dying to know the rest. "Got another?" He went to the refrigerator and rummaged.

"What happened?" I remembered the screams, saw the people racing at least what qualified as racing for oldies. Then there was the Greenjeans and Scissorhands question.

Bob lifted his bottle, slowly unscrewed the top, leaned against the fridge and said, "She liked it."

Fanny exploded. "I don't believe it," she said.

"You've got to be kidding," I said.

"No," Ida said.

"Well, you old son of a gun. Didn't need my Viagras after all," Grady said.

"Who ever said I needed Viagra?" Bob asked.

"And you…" I saw Bob's white round belly, April's elephantine behind, all the other parts I didn't even want to imagine and left the rest of the question unasked.

"And we." Bob showed all of his teeth in a smile so proud and that's when we lost it. Grady and I had to lean on each other for support, Ida started laughing, I think just because we were. It took a while for us to stand upright again.

Fanny, though, wasn't amused. "What'd ya do, shout, 'What? What?' at the critical moment?" Fanny crossed her arms in front of her. She was tapping one little foot on the linoleum.

"Not exactly. But that screaming? Well, that wasn't from fear I can tell you."

"I think I'm going to be sick," Fanny said.

"It certainly drew a crowd." Grady had the look of an adoring frat brother.

"Yeah, that was too bad. April barely got her skirts under control before Mr. Greenjeans came busting in with Mr. Scissorhands close behind. They wrestled me to the floor, but I didn't put up much of a fuss. I'd accomplished my mission."

"Just like a man. Take advantage of an opportunity," Fanny said.

"For the mission, Fanny, for the mission." Bob tossed his empty into the trashcan. He'd worked up quite a thirst.

"So where were you the rest of the day? We've been stuffing those blasted envelopes all afternoon." Fanny was obviously incensed.

"Yeah, Bob, once your wash was done, where'd you go?" Ida asked, bless her heart. She looked around to see if we were going to start laughing again.

"I had to get back to Mrs. B.'s apartment to get those fans. Her son will be by tomorrow early, so I was desperate to get up there, but so was April. So I kept her occupied. Got any crackers?" Bob opened a cabinet.

"You're not telling me you, and April—well, I never!" Ida finally got it.

"All for the mission. She's sleeping it off in my apartment."

"You son of a gun. You must be some stallion," Grady said.

"True, true, but actually it's not what you think. I slipped her a couple of Percodans in a Coke."

Grady looked disappointed. "So did you get the fans?" He pressed.

"Didn't have a chance. Mr. Ramirez was out on his deck fiddling with some invention and I couldn't get past him. It's almost dark now though, so I guess it's safe to go over."

Ida quaked. "I don't think I'd better. I have some baking to do or something."

She waited for dismissal but Fanny let out a short, loud snort. "Don't get the vapors Ida, it's just a quick trip up, then we're finished. We've got the money transferred, disposed of the evidence, stuffed the envelopes. We're in the clear. We need you to help us do a clean sweep of the scene. You don't even have to look at the hag, although the smell might be getting a little thick."

Ida put her hand over her mouth. Her cheeks puffed out and I quickly grabbed the trashcan, but she swallowed hard and we were past the threat.

"Okay," she said. Her voice was anything but confident, but we were in this together. After all, it was her darn brownies that got this ball rolling.

I grabbed Grady's arm and pulled him aside.

"Grady, do you really think Mrs. Berkowitz's son is going to wait until tomorrow to visit his mother after our performance today? He's got to know something is going on." My legs were going all akimbo again. "What if it's too late to get the fans? What if he's up there right now?" I jerked my head in the direction of the dead woman's apartment.

Grady caught my fear. His eyes were wide and staring. "There's only one way to find out." He said, narrowing his eyes. "Let's go."

TWENTY-ONE

IT WAS TIME. Time to get all of this behind us, time to make the 911 call. Time to get back to exercise class, free bread day, and at last, time for me to get to my novel. I wouldn't have any distractions after this, no plots to thicken except on paper, no Bambies to worry about, time to lounge around the pool, eat out of the vending machines, time to imagine what Bob and April really did in the laundry room. Maybe that was taking it a bit too far, but I was certainly ready to appreciate the lifestyle of an Active Senior without the high drama. I said it in my head. *Drama rhymes with jama.*

Grady and I didn't share our fears with the rest of the gang. Didn't want to start a panic. We wanted to believe Mrs. Berkowitz's son would keep his regularly scheduled visit. But what if he didn't?

"Don't the flowers smell lovely?" Ida walked slowly behind Fanny. Her hand looked natural nestled in Grady's, if not a long time in coming. Fanny clinked along, shoving her walker before her, the cloth bag swinging lazily. The sidewalk was alight with luminaries and the cicadas called to one another. A breeze ruffled my hair and awoke quaking aspen. The trees shuddered, sounding like rain. Bob was quietly lumbering slightly ahead of Fanny, his wrinkled shorts higher on the inside of his thighs than on the outside. His white skin glowed in the evening dark. There was no rush; our steps were paced to keep us close enough to touch each other. Our newfound friendship was comfortable, having been strengthened by our shared secrets. We wound our way past the shimmering pool, inviting with its yellow light and the steady hum of its filter puttering along the top of the water. How nice it would be to sit at one of the tables with a glass of wine and a nice steak. I was starving, but we'd talked of going to the Black Angus for a late dinner, so I could wait. I wanted to enjoy the walk, but my nerves were jingling. I hid my shaking hands in my pockets.

We passed Fernon's balcony; his philodendrons were philoden *dones,* all stalk and branches. He held a watering can to the sticks and waved as we passed. His smile was all gums and so beautiful. I returned his wave.

"Wait." Bob stopped short, his beefy arm outstretched like a crossing guard. Fanny nearly tripped over him and kicked his shin. "Gosh darn it, Fanny, that smarts." We all stopped on the sidewalk. I looked around for Mr. Greenjeans, but we were alone on the dusty trail. Not a hide nor hare for miles.

"Listen," Bob said. I listened and groaned. Then I got annoyed. The Mariachis should have closed up shop for the night, and yet the music was playing gleefully across the courtyard. Darn the luck. Now we'll have to sneak past them to get upstairs.

"Wait a minute, Bob, you all have just as much right to go up to my apartment as anybody. We'll just say I'm having you over for tea. He won't be able to tell if you go to my apartment or the one across the landing. It's no big deal."

"She's right," said Grady. "No big deal."

"I wonder how long it will be before we all start acting normally again?" Ida asked, not expecting an answer. That was good because we didn't give her one.

"I can tell when someone is upstairs. I can hear them clomping around, scraping chairs, dropping food. They'll know." Fanny scratched her nose.

"Not if the music is up loud enough." Bob said. I could see the wheels turning.

"I always did enjoy good mariachi music," I said.

"Good, loud mariachi music," Grady said.

"I prefer the classics," Ida said. Bless her heart.

"Whatcha making, Mr. Ramirez?" I nearly had to shout. First there was the music to contend with, then there was Paco cussing me out as only Paco could do, then there was the welder's mask pulled down over Mr. R.'s face. I leaned over the balcony wall and waved. The rest of the Shriners were scuttling up the steps. No need for explanations or requests after all. As far as I could guess, the music was at max decibels.

"Oh hi, May List!" Mr. Mariachi turned down his torch and flipped up the mask. His gold tooth looked blue in the light of the sputtering flame. "Still working on the mail delivery rocket. The last one didn't do so good. I got more powder for this one. Should go a far way." I nodded and smiled. There was still a great deal of confetti around his feet. "Got some connections to do yet, then I'll give it a try tomorrow. By the way, Mrs. Ramirez has tamales for you. You want her to bring them?"

"No! I mean, no thank you, I'll get them tomorrow. Think I'll read a book in the tub and turn in early."

"Okay, don't forget tomorrow is free bread day! Don't be late!" With that he smacked the mask down on his face and went back to work. I glanced over at Bob's apartment before heading up the stairs. Wondered if April would be around for free bread. Good old Bob.

GRADY WAS DOING a quick sweep of the apartment when I got to the crime scene. He came out of the back bedroom and gave me a furtive head nod. We were alone. I sighed with relief.

Ida had her nose pinched and her cheeks puffed again. Fanny was threatening her. "If you blow chunks Ida, I'll toss you over the balcony. They can trace that stuff. Now get busy!" She tossed Ida a paper towel and started wiping stuff down.

"Don't you think that will look a bit strange?" I asked. "No dust, and this woman has been dead for three days?" I looked over at Mrs. Berkowitz. She wasn't shrinking anymore; in fact, she was swelling. Looked like the Michelin man, only a different color.

Grady was probing her while Bob wrapped up the fan cords. "Don't push too hard, Grade, or she might just fly around the room like a balloon." Fanny laughed at that one.

"I've got to get her wallet back into her pocket, but it's tight." Grady pushed again and there was an unmistakable sound. We all looked at each other.

"Oh my god, now she's passing wind. As if this room wasn't reeking enough as it is," Fanny said. She waved an arthritic hand in front of her face. "May. Get over here and get some tinfoil. We've got to fix that back window." I hurried to comply. Anything to finish up.

"Grady, what about the safety deposit key? I almost forgot."

"It's back where I found it." He looked at Fanny. "Clean of prints. There's nothing to do about that; let her son have it for all I care."

Bob came back a bit breathless. "Fans are back at your place, May. Are we all set?" We all nodded. Bob ticked off the inventory. Floors vacuumed, surfaces wiped down, key back in the aquarium, wallet in the pocket, accounts transferred, envelopes stuffed, April asleep downstairs with her master key in the bottom of her purse. I slowly thumbed the light off and we became shadows.

"Have we forgotten anything?" Bob spoke through the dark.

"Only one thing," said a deep voice I didn't recognize. The balcony screen door slid open. Ida screamed and pressed herself to Grady's back. We stared at the dark form coming into Mrs. Berkowitz's living room. Grady put a protective hand on Ida's hip. I clutched Fanny, Bob clutched me, and none of us could utter a word. I should say not any word that made sense. Ida was trying hard for an encore but she'd spent all her breath on the first outburst and was hyperventilating again.

"I can see you have a gun," Grady said, matter of factly, but his voice was strained.

"Nine mike-mike," Fanny confirmed.

"Woooo, I just soiled my Depends," Ida cried.

"It's okay, Ida, we'll get a new one later," Grady consoled.

The man came into view, the contours of his face taking form in the parking lot's security light. My eyes had gotten used to the dark and I recognized him as Mr. Hansom. Mrs. Berkowitz's ex-P.I., ex-extortionist, ex-banker son.

"Missed the balcony," Grady whispered apologetically.

"I thought it was awfully strange to see my dead mother walk into the bank today," Mr. Hansom said. He was holding the gun at waist level and approaching one slow step at a time. We matched him step for step, moving backwards, a huddled mass of soiling, quaking, blubbering blue hairs. "I thought it was even more odd when I got up here a few minutes ago and found her resting so serenely on the couch. I could have *sworn* I left her on the floor." Another step. "And when I checked her computer, guess what? Someone has erased all of her accounts. Now isn't that strange?" Step, step.

We were backed up to the coffee table. Mr. Hansom pushed the barrel of the gun against Grady's chin. Grady's nostrils were flaring, but he stared straight into Mr. Hansom's face. Ida turned her head and threw up on the glove doilies.

"Sorry," she peeped.

"'S awright Ida," Grady said, without breaking his stare.

"For a minute I thought I'd lost my mind," Mr. Hansom said. He moved the pistol over to me and took a bead. My upper lip was getting moist but I didn't dare make a move to wipe. "What would you think if you saw your dead mother walking around, and then found her taking a cozy rest in the breeze of two box fans?"

"Those were hers," Fanny said jerking her head my way. I popped my mouth open and gave her a look. "They were," she said.

Mr. Hansom pushed the gun back under Grady's neck. "I know you. I saw you today at the bank. Couldn't remember at first, but then I thought about it. Saw your face here a couple of times when I picked up my mother. And now here we are. Aren't we a snug little party?"

Mr. H. leaned around Grady and pushed at Ida's hair with the gun barrel. "And who had the bright idea to bring my mother brownies the other day? You know she's insulin dependent don't you? Too much sugar and she, well, she ends up like that." The man waved the gun at the couch.

"It was her idea," Fanny said, looking at me.

"Fanny!" I said.

"Well, it was."

"Then it's you I have to thank. Couldn't come up with really good idea, but when I saw the plate of brownies on her counter it was just perfect. Fill her with enough insulin to drop a giraffe, put a little brownie around her mouth and dump the rest. It's pretty hard to eat when you're dead." The man rubbed the gun under his chin, pleased with himself.

"Ah ah! *You* killed her!" Fanny broke away from the pack and lifted her walker. It was the last thing Mr. Hansom expected. She wiggled so fast it looked like a shudder, swung the metal cage in an arc, and cold-cocked the son of Mrs. Berkowitz. It even sounded like a nine iron striking pay dirt. "Fore!" She shouted after the fact, pounced on the fallen Mr. H, and dug her knee into his jugular. "Don't just stand there you bunch of drooling fools, grab the gun!"

Elbows, knees, dentures, hearing aids, Depends, all in a writhing mass, scrambled for the gun. There was plenty of swearing and grunting going on, I took a fin-gernail in the eye, but when it was over Bob had the gun, and Grady had taken over for Fanny. He held Mr. H. while she used the telephone cord to wrap his hands and feet together in whipping loops. Then she jumped up with her arms held high. I'd seen a cowboy make that move at a rodeo once. He was good. She was better.

We were panting, standing in a circle around the struggling murderer, wondering what we should do with him, when an explosion shook the floor. Wood splintered, clattered, and pelted the outside wall. Mr. H. could wait. We ran to the balcony wondering what added catastrophe could make our situation any worse than it already was.

"Earthquake?" Bob asked.

"Mr. Ramirez," Fanny said.

"Mr. Ramirez?" I looked over the railing and noticed the stairs that should have gone from the floor to my apartment—didn't. There was only a dark hole where they had been. Newspaper litter gently fluttered down onto my hair, turning the evening into a winter wonderland.

I couldn't help myself. I started to laugh hard. I turned my face to the sky and let the paper snow dot my tongue. "Are you alright, Mr. Ramirez?" I called down after spitting out a few wads.

"I'm alright, I'm okay, think I got too much powder. Sorry about your stairs, May List."

I laughed harder and shook the snow from my hair.

"Uh, Mr. Ramirez, I think your house is on fire." Grady leaned over the railing beside me and pointed. There were little orange flames creeping up his drapes. I could hear Mrs. Mariachi yelling what was probably profanity, but I couldn't be sure. I didn't speak that language. It all happened so fast. Mr. Greenjeans came running, fire trucks wailed in the distance, April stumbled out of Bob's apartment and shouted, "What? What?" The whole body of Active Seniors poured from their caves and stood in bathrobes, slippers and curlers, pointing and craning. The air was thick with liniment and cold cream. Mr. Scissorhands came running with a fire extinguisher, stumbled and fumbled, hit the pavement and doused the screaming throng in white foam. Geriatrics scattered.

Mr. Greenjeans waved his arms around and signaled the fire trucks to hoist a ladder so the old folks could be rescued. Paco barked non-stop. I guess this really was an Active Senior Living complex after all. The first fireman came across the late Mrs. Berkowitz's balcony and gingerly took Ida's hand, then got a whiff of Mrs. B. and called in the paramedics. Fanny waved off all help and vaulted over the rail. Bob, Grady and I waited for the signal to go.

"I'll stay and explain everything to the police when they get here," Grady said.

"Almost everything," Bob corrected, and wandered off to raid the fridge.

"Just wondering," I said, bending down to look Mr. H. in the face. "What did you do with the brownies?"

"Garbage disposal," he grumbled. "That much chocolate will kill ya."

The next person over the balcony and into the apartment wasn't a fireman, it was Mr. Greenjeans. He walked confidently into the living room and didn't seem at all surprised to see a man tied up on the floor, but he was a bit curious about the bloated Mrs. Berkowitz. He reached into his pocket and produced a badge.

"My name is Frank Billings. I've been working undercover for weeks trying to pin down this guy. Thanks for holding him for me."

My gut twisted. "What for, Mr. Green…um, Mr. Billings, what has he done?"

"Tax evasion, grand theft auto, outstanding warrants all over the place but he's pretty slick. I've been staking out the place here trying to catch up with him. I've never known anyone who could get in and out of places without being seen as well as this guy."

"Not too hard if you've got the right outfit." Bob's voice.

It was more than my legs could handle. All of the tension, excitement, sheer terror of the evening did me in and I slumped to the floor. There in the hallway was Mrs. Berkowitz: Pippi Longstocking hair, Picasso makeup, spike heels, but no, this Mrs. B was huge. It just magnified the horror of it. She's back!

"Bob. What are you doing?" Grady had gone through the shock and was into the incredulous stage.

"She never left her apartment. Mrs. Berkowitz never left her apartment. He probably wore her stuff over here half the time. That's why nobody spotted him, and it's how he walked right under your nose again and again." Bob pointed the wig at Mr. Greenjeans/detective.

This guy's name's Sam Berkowitz."

Mr. H. turned his face toward the wall.

"Yeah, I recognize him. We've been doing a pretty thorough investigation for way more hours than I'd like to admit," Mr. Billings said.

"What did you find?" Grady's voice was a bit too high.

"Just one little thing, but something big enough to put him away for a long time. Got a search warrant for a safety deposit box he had in his name, along with his mother's. Got into it today with the permission of the bank. We had a feeling he was getting ready to cut out of here tomorrow."

"What was in it?" Bob asked.

"Life insurance policies taken out on his mother. Lots, over a short period of time, with different companies. My guess is that, er, woman over there didn't die of natural causes. Just too bad you didn't find her sooner. Could have saved us a lot of time."

TWENTY-TWO

The Black Angus was near closing time when the Shriners sat down to a beef feast. We touched wine glasses and toasted the mission.

"Speaking of which," Fanny said, "after we give back all of the money to those still living, how much is left for the benevolent cause?"

Grady stroked his chin, and I swear I saw his eyes sparkle. Ida had a new change of Depends in which she squirmed like a schoolgirl. Fanny held her hands out; Bob leaned back in his chair and folded his napkin.

"Enough to turn the Active Senior Living complex into a resort."

"Could we get bowling alleys?" Ida asked. She was practically bouncing in her chair, overtaken by the excitement.

"And a golf course?" Fanny asked. She put her hands together as if in prayer, imagining the possibilities.

"And slot machines?" That was Bob.

"That and then some." Grady sipped his wine.

As we reveled in our good fortune, Grady filled in some of the details about Mrs. B. and her degenerate son. Mr. Greenjeans was quite open with his informa-

tion, especially after Grady hinted that he knew something about the detective's frequent hotel visits at the
local rent-by-the-hour establishment. (Mrs. B. wasn't
the only one who gathered *data*.)

We had been right in our assumptions that the
younger Berkowitz had been the head that had turned
the arthritic extortionist's neck. He'd worked hard to
get the personal dirt on all of the old timers over the
years. Mrs. Berkowitz would check into an apartment
complex, trailer park, nursing home, wherever, and in
a couple of years she'd had nearly all of them in her
back pocket. Only thing was, the young Mr. B. didn't
have a whole lot of love for his aging mom; in fact, he
was piling up life insurance policies with the hopes that
she'd knock off after he amassed a sizeable fortune.
When it looked like she was as healthy as ever, he grew
impatient. He started getting concerned when her
mental capacities started to go, and he worried that she
would slip up, exposing him for what he was.

"So he decided to whack her with an extra large
helping of insulin," Bob summarized. "Apparently she
didn't feel a thing. Just turned around, and jab. All
done." Grady motioned with his fork. "Then he figured
he'd get all of the paperwork tidied up, go back to her
apartment, call 911 and tell them she'd eaten all of the
brownies. It took him longer to get on with the bank.
Good thing for us, too, or it would have been a wash."

"Boy was he stupid," Fanny huffed. "All they had
to do was order an autopsy and examine her stomach

contents. Do some blood work, serum samples. That story would have crumbled like Ida's bundt cake."

The comment seemed to go right over Ida's head. She was probably thinking about her bowling alley.

"He thought of that," Grady continued. "Generally they only order autopsies if something looks wrong, like a murder, or suicide, or, you know, something suspicious. Nothing too unusual about a ninety-year-old woman dead on the floor of her apartment. Happens all the time. To cover his bets, though, her son was prepared to order a quick cremation."

"So she really was murdered, after all." Ida said quietly. "Mr. Greenjeans, er, the detective, is a slick guy. He got Mrs. B.'s son to cop a plea almost before he had him cuffed and in the squad car. Mr. Hansom, or whatever his name is, knew we'd roll over. With all of the other charges against him, he was squealing like a stuck pig. He admitted the whole thing."

"The whole thing?" Ida looked worried.

"Except for the money. Why add another charge to his already mounting allegations? If he's like most of the arrogant sociopaths I've heard of, he's thinking he'll beat the wrap and come back to get the money," Grady said.

"Oh Lordy!" Ida gasped. "Let's hope he doesn't wrap the beet. What would he do to us?"

"Don't give it another thought, Ida. If he comes calling, we'll just invite him in for cookies," Fanny said.

"That's not very nice." Ida scowled.

"Bob," I said, "what about you? What did our beloved Mrs. B. have on you?" In my other life I would have probed delicately, danced around the question, I would have drawn him out using psychology and ploys, but that was then. I went straight for the jugular. "Hmm?"

Bob was caught off guard. He had a mouth full of spinach. He'd already stained the front of his white shirt with A-1 sauce and he still had half a steer on his plate.

"Yeah, Bob, I saw the data sheet. Something to do with a little *arson* project?" Fanny threw a bread stick at him. It landed in his water glass. Bob stuck his thick fingers in and fished out the stick. Then he sucked the end of it. Still, he wasn't talking.

"It's okay, Bob. You don't have to tell." Mother Ida speaking.

"Spill it, Bob," Grady said.

Bob dug at his teeth with a fingernail. Then he took a drink of wine. Then he wiped his mouth with the back of his hand. He was taking his time.

"Come on, Bob," I said.

Bob lifted the candle from the middle of the table and waved a finger through its flame. "Remember Yellowstone? '88? Big fire?" he asked.

"Yeah, burned hundreds of acres," I said, not knowing where this could be going.

Bob replaced the candle. "That was me." He bit off the end of the bread and chewed.

"That was you?" I quickly looked over my left

shoulder, then my right and hissed. "You started the Yellowstone fire?"

"Oh no, no, no, May Bell," Ida corrected. "Bob was the San Dimas fire chief around that time. He would have been *fighting* the fire."

I rubbed my temples and did some math. First of all, I didn't think they would send old men to fight fires; secondly, he wouldn't go from being the fire chief in San Dimas to being a smoke jumper in Wyoming; and third, that would have merited him a badge of honor. Not a place on the Mrs. Berkowitz file.

"No, May was right. I started the fire."

"But why?" Ida's eyes were gigantic.

"Things were getting a *little* boring. I wanted to see how the big boys did things. Unfortunately, well, it got a little out of hand." Bob cleared his throat.

"A little out of hand? A little out of hand?" I didn't know what else to say.

"They never knew how it started, exactly, but a couple of campers saw me and reported it to the ranger station. Not long after that, I started getting a little weird, just to throw them off. I started wearing skirts around the fire station and they retired me early. Cops filed a report, asked me questions, but by that time I could only say two words. And they let it go."

"Two words?" I said.

"What? What?" Bob put his hands in the air.

Fanny drummed her hands on the table and laughed so hard she snorted.

"Gee, Bob," Grady said. "I hope you got it out of your system. California ain't that big."

I caught a half-smile playing along Grady's mouth. Ida giggled too.

"Imagine," Fanny said, "there goes the fire chief, and oh, look! Today he's wearing the Christian Dior, full pleated skirt. And there he goes, riding along on the back of that beautiful red fire truck. Doesn't it make a pretty picture?"

It was sick, but the image of Bob riding along the back of a wailing fire truck with his skirts whipping around his huge thighs caused the bubble to work its way up my throat again and I joined Ida. We were all laughing like kids when the waiter came to take our dessert order.

Most of the customers had gone, so we asked for more wine, forget the dessert; one more for the road and we were outta there. The waiter was gracious. I hoped it was genuine and he wasn't doing anything to our drinks behind the kitchen doors.

"Okay, Ida, your turn." Bob rubbed his nose and pointed a bread stick her way.

Ida looked startled and waved her hands in front of her face. "Never you mind. Just don't worry about it, forget it," she said.

Fanny crossed her arms and scowled. "Listen miss fancy pants. It wouldn't be too hard for us to find out. May here told us about her bigotry."

"Bigamy," I said quickly, and then cringed. "Bob told us about trying to burn down Wyoming."

"And a bit of Montana, too," Bob said. He was flicking sesame seeds off a roll.

"We know Grady got in over his head with cheap sunglasses, and that I posted my husband at the Petersons', but you, missy, have kept your lips buttoned. Now fess up.

We've spilled our guts, so who are you to think you're better than us?"

"Ease up, Fanny," Grady said. He touched Ida's hand. "I'll tell it if you want, honey."

"Honey?" Bob and I exchanged a look.

"No. I'll tell it." Ida straightened in her chair and lifted the napkin off her lap. She dabbed, placed the napkin on the table and began.

"When I started teaching I was only twenty-one. I had a lot of ideas about the way things should be. I didn't exactly go along with the status crow."

"Imagine that. Ida—a mover and a shaker," Fanny gouged.

"Shut up, Fanny," we said.

"There was a little boy in my class. His name was Jimmy Donovan. Smart enough kid, a little too talkative sometimes, didn't like to sit still much, but what ten-year-old does? I just fell in love with that boy. Sweet, innocent, always polite and kind. He'd stay behind after class to help me clean up most days, and after a while I began to wonder why he wasn't hurrying to get home like the rest of the kids. They couldn't wait to get out of there as soon as the last bell rang."

"Trouble on the home front?" I guessed.

"It took me quite a while to figure it out. One day, though, I asked him to get some supplies out of the closet. I was putting together a St. Patrick's Day poster and needed construction paper, poster board, that kind of stuff. He wouldn't do it. I asked him a second time, and even took him to the closet to show him where everything was, but he looked positively terrified."

"Of construction paper?" Fanny looked incredulous.

"Of the closet." Ida sounded pained. "He told me then, that his parents sometimes put him in his bedroom closet when he was hyperactivated."

"Oh my gosh." I shook my head. "How horrible."

"I told him it was okay, that I would take care of the poster and sent him home. But I was getting really angry. In those days you just didn't interfere with a parent's disciplinary means, but this was too much."

"So you reported them. Right?"

"To whom? Remember, this was years and years ago. We just didn't have the agencies that we have today. No, I decided I'd handle it on my own."

"You? What did you do, bake them some brownies?" Fanny jabbed again.

"Very funny," Ida said. "The next week was parent-teacher conferences. I scheduled them first on my appointment calendar. They were right on time, all smiling, shaking my hand, all the while checking their watches, because they had other things to do that day.

I showed them around the room, pointed out the things their son had done, told them how wonderful he was, then I showed them to the closet."

"You mean you showed them the closet," Bob said.

"No, I showed them *to* the closet. I led them in, turned, and then *locked* them in."

"Ida?" I was amazed.

"I held the rest of my conferences outside. It was a beautiful day, and nobody could hear the banging or shouts from the lawn. The other teachers didn't hear a thing. That was one sturdy schoolhouse." Ida smiled, reveling in the memory. "I released them about six hours later. They were ready to kill me by that time, but I gave them a lecture about their son and pushed them out the door."

"They filed a complaint, didn't they?" I asked.

"My word against theirs." Ida said. "Still, it hung over my head for quite a while. Luckily my reputation was stellar, while they weren't quite the popular couple in their neighborhood and it eventually all went away."

"How was Mrs. Berkowitz able to use this?" I asked.

"When I got my letter, she told me the couple had been found, and that they were ready to sue me for something called post-dramatic stretch syndrome, or something like that. I guess they never got over it."

"Oh, Ida." I shook my head. Poor thing, what a ruse. There was no way Mrs. Berkowitz could drum up a real case. She had a lot of wicked ways, that one.

It had worked, because Ida had been forking over cash for nearly three years.

"On behalf of little Jimmy Donovan, here's to you." I lifted my glass.

"Here, here." The rest of the gang lifted theirs in a toast.

Grady grew quiet suddenly, and looked over my shoulder with a look of surprise. Everyone just sort of paused, and then looked at me, staring in a strange expectant way.

"May?" A voice I recognized well, spoke softly behind me. I looked at everyone, saw their unusual reactions, but their faces were unreadable.

"Can I talk with you, May?" I didn't want to look at him, I wanted to give him a scissor, send him on his way, kick his Luv Macheen all the way back to Ohio. I looked at him.

Ted. He was standing behind me, the vision of a defeated man. His clothes were rumpled; his shoulders slumped, not like the Ted I had left in Ohio. Everyone was uneasy, looking at their plates, and since I didn't care to discuss my personal life in front of them, I lifted my wine glass and stood up.

"Let's get another table," I said. I apologized to the others and walked with Ted to a quiet corner. I sat down with my glass of wine and watched as he slid into a chair across from me. My hands were shaking, my knees were shaking, and I waited.

"I've been looking all over for you since you left."

"How did you track me down?" I wanted to sound firm and I did sound firm. It was scary. I didn't want to look at him. My finger circled the top of my wine glass.

"Your driver's license, the license plates of my car. I haven't slept since you left. I've been looking for you everywhere. Why did you leave me, May?"

I wasn't falling for it. The quivering chin, the dark circles, the sad eyes. "I know about you and the other women. Gone all the time, rushing out in the middle of the night, surrounded by nurses all day. I know, and don't you think I don't, because I do." Now my chin was quivering.

"May, I'm a doctor."

"So? That gives you an excuse to fool around?"

"May, I love you. I haven't been with anyone else."

"Well, okay, then explain the time I heard you on the phone singing 'Luv Mucheen.' Huh mister? Explain that! And if you pause for a second, I'll know you're lying."

"Luv Mucheen?" He paused.

"See? I knew you'd lie about it."

Ted started to laugh and took my hands in his. I didn't pull away, but thought about lifting the glass with my teeth. I needed a drink.

"That was a late night call-in radio program. I was trying to win you a trip to Hawaii. See?" Ted dug around in his wallet and produced a crumpled letter from the radio station. "I didn't win, but I got us a weekend at a B & B in Huber Heights." He looked hopeful.

I grabbed the letter. It was official.

"You don't have to win me a trip to Hawaii, Ted. We can afford that." I was talking in present tense. Uh oh. Slipping ever so easily under his spell.

"It's just the competitor in me. You know how I am—always have to be the best, the smartest, work the longest hours. May, I owe you an apology. I've let my job become more important than you. This was a wakeup call for me, and I've decided, if you come home, I'll quit my practice."

I looked for strength from my Shriner friends, but they were talking, probably planning their new real estate investment.

"There's something I have to tell you, Ted." I closed my eyes. "I was already married when I married you." I opened one eye a little and saw him looking at me with a tender expression.

"I know, May. I've known all along."

"What?" I jerked my hands away.

"I always wanted to tell you this." Ted cleared his throat, apparently looking for the words. "I knew your first husband. We met on a bus to basic training during the Korean War. We were both from Ohio and had a lot in common. Later, after my medic training, I was assigned to his unit. He was in ordnance and I just tagged along to patch up the guys who weren't lucky enough to avoid the inevitable tragedies of war. Your first husband and I got really close. He had a picture of you in his wallet and talked about you all the time.

He loved you very much, couldn't say enough good things about you, and before long, I was falling in love with the beautiful woman in the picture."

I was aghast. I knew Ted had spent some time in Korea but he talked about it very little. No wonder. "If he loved me so much, why did he leave me?" I had come to believe the Berkowitz report. She'd been right about everything else, why break tradition?

"May, I hate to tell you this, but your first husband, I don't know how to say it except in medical terms, he stepped on a land mine and…"

"He was killed?" Ah hah! So he was dead after all. I knew it. Mrs. B. had been wrong this time!

"He had his manhood altered," Ted said.

"He what?"

"Lost his boys."

"He had his giblets blown off?"

"That's another way of putting it. He continued to talk about you, even in his pain. Said he couldn't go back to you because you'd never divorce him, you were that loyal, and he couldn't be a husband to you. I would just listen and listen, while I packed ice around the lesion."

"You iced down his…"

"I think he's in Tibet now, said he was joining a monastery. But I fell in love with you before I ever saw you. I tracked you down that time and I tracked you down this time and I'm asking you to come home."

I gave him a long time to squirm. I told him how

wonderful my apartment was, how far I'd come on my book, how great the exercise class made me feel—he agreed I looked pretty good with my newer, slimmer body—and then I threw myself across the table and begged him to take me out of there.

I VISIT THE COMPLEX once in a while when Ted and I are en route to Mexico, or Belize, or Los Angeles. There's a new apartment manager, his name is Brad-Lance and I hear he's doing a fine job overseeing the polo matches, the salons and mud baths, the live entertainment and the slot machines. Grady and Ida now share a condo in the senior marrieds' section; Bob teaches tap, jazz and ballet; and Fanny moved out to live with her forensic buddy. I hear she's the senior pro at the complex and tees up every morning before six. April went to work for Maytag, Mr. Greenjeans retired his coveralls, and Mr. Scissorhands scissored a lion at the zoo and is no longer with us.

Ida started taking cooking classes last week.

Care for a brownie?